Murder
Crossed

A   H E N R Y   H O L T   M Y S T E R Y

ALSO BY ELEANOR BOYLAN

A HENRY HOLT MYSTERY

Murder Crossed

ELEANOR BOYLAN

Henry Holt and Company • New York

Henry Holt and Company, Inc.
Publishers since 1866
115 West 18th Street
New York, New York 10011

Henry Holt® is a registered trademark of
Henry Holt and Company, Inc.

Library of Congress Cataloging-in-Publication Data

Boylan, Eleanor.
Murder crossed/Eleanor Boylan.—1st ed.
p.   cm.—(A Henry Holt mystery)
I. Title.
PS3552.0912M78   1996   95–34659
813'.54—dc20   CIP
ISBN 0-8050-3922-8

Henry Holt books are available for special
promotions and premiums. For details contact:
Director, Special Markets.

First Edition—1996

Designed by Paula R. Szafranski

Printed in the United States of America
All first editions are printed on acid-free paper. ∞

1   3   5   7   9   10   8   6   4   2

Murder
Crossed

A H E N R Y H O L T M Y S T E R Y

1

I must take you back three months, gestation time for the murder, the same number of months, I'm told, as for a tiger. Grimly appropriate.

It was conceived on a breezy March day in the town of Woolcott, Massachusetts, and though one might have wished for a miscarriage, the thing went full term and was born, bouncing and terrible, the following June.

My cousin Charles Saddlier, known to family and friends as Sadd, values literate expression above life itself and thinks I've carried the above metaphor too far; but I like it because there were children involved, three little girls whom my daughter, Paula, called "the beanbags." Certainly they were tossed about, poor mites, but when your mother is a famous movie star, you can't expect to have the childhood of Meg, Jo, Beth, and Amy.

Now to take you back those three months.

Woolcott is a pleasant suburb of Boston where I spent four teenage years at Woolcott Academy. This small, first-rate, rather obscure boarding school for girls has survived chiefly owing to its excellence and a militantly loyal alumnae. In this era, which has seen the closing of so many private schools, "Wooly," as it is affectionately known—and its students as "Woolies"—has gone stoutly on educating our daughters and granddaughters and as stoutly remaining an all-girl school. Twenty years ago when Paula graduated, the headmistress, or rather the Head (I struggled valiantly to keep up with the times), herself a granddaughter of the school's founder, said in her commencement address: "We simply believe that a young woman can study better when seated in class beside another young woman rather than a young man."

Conservative almost to the point of being reactionary, Woolcott Academy is the kind of school that girls complain about being sent to, then proceed to send their daughters.

"I'm dying of curiosity," said Paula on that March morning as we sat, I still in my bathrobe, on her rather sagging front porch. Her two cats squatted on the rickety rail. Paula and her husband, Andy, had bought a big, old "fixer-upper" in the Boston suburb of Dedham and were blithely not fixing it up. "Louise wouldn't tell me a thing on the phone except that she wanted to see you and was sending you this letter." She pulled an envelope from the morning mail. "Do you know how to get there?"

"Get to Wooly?" I looked at my daughter in surprise.

"I mean, some of the exits have been changed." Paula took her sneakered feet from the rail, and both cats clawed into it as it swayed. "When 95 went in it screwed up a lot of old exits. Woolcott is exit number 53 now."

"Oh. Thanks. Will an hour do it from here?"

"Less. I'll get more coffee."

Paula went into the house, and I opened the letter. There was a folded enclosure that appeared to be another letter in enormous handwriting. I opened Louise Littleton's typewritten one first. It was on familiar Woolcott Academy stationery and engraved "Office of the Principal." It read:

Dear Mrs. Gamadge:

You were out when I called Paula, but I was delighted to learn that you were visiting her. She said you'd come up to see her new house. How lucky for me! I'd called to get your phone number in New York, but now I can ask for your help in person. That is, if you can spare the time to come see me. I'm told you often advise people in difficult situations, and as an "old Wooly" your opinion will be especially valuable to me.

I'm typing this letter myself because I don't want my secretary to know about it. She's a dear soul and very good at her job, but she's also Cuban and excitable. I'm afraid she'd be *very* excited by the enclosed. Fortunately, it was marked "Personal" and came to my desk unopened. By the way, doesn't it sound exactly like the writer?

I'd be so grateful if you could come before Thursday. I don't want D. arriving before I've had a chance to talk to you. And don't bother to call; just come at any hour.

Many thanks,
Louise Littleton

I unfolded the enclosure. It was the antithesis of the other letter. The writing sprawled and slanted across pinkish lavender paper, and it was full of underlinings and scratched-out words. I had the odd feeling of almost having to hold it down to calm it as I read it.

Darling Lou,

I know! I know! You're saying to yourself how does she have the nerve after all the years and all the awfulness, but oh, Lou, I'm desperate and I need you so badly! I'm in Boston and I'm not going to phone you because

I'm scared you'd hang up, so I'm just arriving at Wooly on Thursday, and for God's sake please, *please* see me and hear me, my dear, darling friend.

Duff

The thing affected me as it had undoubtedly affected Louise Littleton. I felt a breathlessness combined with bafflement and curiosity to which, in her case, must have been added an element of dread.

Paula came back with two cups of her rather awful coffee; she's a terrible cook, and her husband is a superb one. Andy Fortina's parents were born in Brazil, and his sauces . . . !

I said, extending the letters, "The name Duff will ring a bell."

Paula stared at me. "You mean . . . ?"

I nodded. She gave me a cup, took the letters, and sat down, devouring the contents of both.

It was fascinating but sad to consider the identity—and yet the gulf—between Elaine Duffy, charity pupil at Woolcott Academy twenty-five years ago, and superstar Margo Llewelyn, who, with her shiny new name, shot to the heights of "filmdom" (Sadd says there's no such word) in the seventies and eighties. In the delightful tradition of Carole Lombard and Kay Kendall, names that come to me from my own generation, she was lovely and funny, that rare thing, the beautiful comedian. But gradually and tragically, her fate had closed in. Now in her forties and racked by a life of dissipation and wildly inappropriate marriages, her professional reputation was in shreds and she hadn't made a movie in several years. Too often difficult, drunk, and demoralized, she was, according to gossip, unhireable.

And she was about to descend on her old friend and classmate, Louise Littleton, highly respected Head of Woolcott Academy. No wonder Louise was quailing.

Paula folded both letters with a "Wow!"

I said, "Help me with chronology. How much older is she than you?"

"Four or five years. She and Louise were graduating when I was in the ninth grade. Both of them had started in the Lower School when they were just little kids."

I took the letters from Paula. "I remember you telling me they were good friends."

"Yes. The best. All those years. And it was funny because they were so different. Lou—and Duff was the only girl in the school who could get away with calling her that—Lou came from some snooty Philadelphia clan, and Duff had no family at all. The rumor was that her mother had been a maid in the school." Paula pulled one of the cats into her lap. "You and Dad used to come to Wooly a lot my first year. Did you ever see Duff?"

"Not that I remember. And it wasn't until she got famous that you began talking about her."

Paula nodded. "And remembering things. She was so gorgeous—blond, of course—and she got lousy marks and was always in trouble. Louise was the perfect lady and a brain. She wasn't bad looking herself, but Duff just put everybody in the shade. A lot of the girls hated her, but in some weird way, she and Louise hit it off."

I stared out at the brown lawn. Paula held the cat against her cheek and went on

"Everybody knew they had one thing in common—neither of them had parents. Louise's grandparents were quote unquote 'raising her,' which meant they threw her in Wooly when she was seven or eight." She laughed. "Once in a while they'd drive up from Philly in their Rolls to see her, and we'd all hang out of the window to look at it. Nobody ever came to see Duff."

We were silent for a moment. A breeze stirred the about-to-burst forsythia bush beside the porch.

Then I said, "What was Louise's maiden name?"

"Archer. That was sad. The year she graduated from Bryn Mawr she married Brad Littleton who taught at Wooly, and he was killed in Cambodia six months later. She went back to Wooly as a teacher and she's devoted her life to it." Paula drained her coffee cup and looked back at the pink letter. "She's right. This does sound like Duff. Crazy wild from day one. What do you suppose she wants?"

"We may never find out."

"Why?"

"I have a feeling Louise will get cold feet at the last minute and decide to be away. Simpler just to leave a message: 'Sorry, called away on business.' "

"Oh, that would be rotten! Duff sounds so desperate."

"All the more reason. Forget Duff for a minute. Doesn't Margo Llewelyn have children?"

Paula regarded me for an instant, then grinned. "She sure does! Two or three, I think. And as many husbands—maybe more—who can count?" Paula grasped her brow and hooted. "Wait! At least one of her kids is a girl—I'm sure of it! Oh, Mom, this is rich! You don't suppose she wants to put her in Wooly!"

"I could be totally wrong." I tucked the letters in my bathrobe pocket. "Maybe Margo Llewelyn just wants to decide whether to endow her alma mater now or later."

"Oh, sure!" Paula was hugging herself. "Can't you just picture it? Margo whirling in on Visiting Day, having alerted the press, of course, that she is doing her maternal duty."

"And insisting," I couldn't help adding, "that her picture be taken with her dear old friend, Louise Littleton—"

"—who would just die at this kind of publicity! I love it!" Paula stood up. "All I can say is get out there quick, and hey"—she snapped her fingers—"didn't she say come before Thursday? This is Wednesday!"

"I better get dressed." I stood up.

"Shall I call Louise and say you're coming?"

"She said not to. What time is it?"

"Almost nine. Gotta get to work." She hugged me. "Watch out for those boxes in the upstairs hall." (I'd tripped over them twice already.) "One of these days I'm going to unpack 'em, I swear it." She cupped my face. "In spite of all the booby traps, you do like our house, don't you?"

"I love it."

"It's a rambling wreck, but so are we." Paula took her shoulder bag from the chair back and ran down the creaking steps.

I called, "Do you go to work in sneakers?"

"Why not?"

And seconds later, the blue and white van backed precipitously out of the rutted driveway and disappeared.

Paula worked in the office of her children's grade school. At about three o'clock the van would wheel in again carrying third grader Janey and kindergartner Andrea. Then there would be bedlam till the arrival of their father, usually bearing an armload of metal film containers. "Vintage Flicks" was Andy's shop/studio in South Boston where he wallowed happily in the cutting, mending, sorting, splicing, trading, and God-knows-whating of old films, making a living, thank heaven, and coming home to make wonderful family meals. Afterward, Paula more or less cheerfully tackled the kitchen—anything was better than cooking to her—and Andy would betake himself to his "basement office" (a badly lit cellar) to continue cutting, sorting, splicing, etc. Janey and Andrea simply circulated constantly, as did the cats. On weekends, as far as I could see, when the fixer-upper should be getting fixed up, Paula preferred to play indoor tennis, and rotund Andy, who loathed exercise, preferred to cook, or to cut, sort, and splice. .

The ménage, to my satisfaction, seemed a contented one.

I walked up the long bare stairs of the house, the words of

Margo Llewelyn's letter running in my mind. "I know! You're saying to yourself . . . but oh, Lou, I'm desperate. . . . *Please* see me and hear me."

I was scouring the grubby bathtub and praying for enough hot water, when the phone rang. Picking my way around the packing boxes, I reached Paula and Andy's room and plucked the phone from the unmade bed.

"Paula?"

"No, this is her—"

"Mrs. Gamadge!" The voice was unmistakably that of someone with a bad cold. "Your voices are so alike! This is Louise Littleton."

"Louise," I said, "I've just gotten your letter, and I'm dressing to come see you."

"Oh, thank heaven! Oh, that's wonderful! Oh, I'm so relieved!" Three "Oh's" in three sentences. Anxious? Ill? Then, "Oh, thank you!" The fourth "Oh" was followed by a violent sneeze.

"You have a bad cold," I said.

"Yes, the kind that won't quit." A nervous laugh. "Has Paula told you about the new exit number?"

"She has, and I'll see you in about an hour and a half."

Another sneeze blurred her continued thanks, and I hung up.

We city dwellers are always glad of an excuse to rent a car. I'd picked this one up at the airport and had been enjoying tooling around the Boston suburbs with my grandchildren, conscientiously remembering to strap them in, while recalling guiltily how my own children would roll around in the back of a station wagon. When tempted to deplore certain aspects of modern civilization, I try to think of things like compulsory seat belts for babies' car seats. We can't be all bad.

Again, bits of that letter came to me as I sailed down Route 95. "I'm in Boston." Odd that the media hadn't mentioned it. Was Margo Llewelyn so pathetically passé that there would be no interest? Not possible. The public adores a spectacle of disintegration among its icons. No, she must have taken pains to come in quietly, even anonymously.

I got off the highway at Exit 53, thinking of her children. Where were they? Where they always were, I supposed, in various lush and lonely spots with everything money could buy and in need of everything it couldn't, vied for, wrangled over, cut, sorted, and spliced . . .

Did Louise Littleton suspect, as I did, what she was to "please, *please* . . . hear" and its ramifications? Not exactly a thought to improve one's morale—or one's cold.

2

O f course that's what she wants!"
Louise buried her face in a tissue, blew her nose, and looked at me with rheumy, troubled eyes.

I said, "We may be jumping to conclusions, Louise."

"No, we're not." A miserable shake of the head.

"Wouldn't it be kind to see her—for old times' sake at least?"

Louise groaned, and the phone on her desk rang. She said congestedly, "Excuse be" and picked up the receiver. While she listened, spoke, and nodded wearily, I looked around the familiar precincts.

The Woolcott Academy of my day was ancient history, and even Paula's day was long past. Nothing was the same—with one exception: the "Head'"s house.

The nineteenth-century fieldstone structure in which we sat had been the gatehouse for the no-longer-existing mansion that was the original school. Over the decades, classrooms, dormitories, a science building, a gym, a pool—even a skating rink—had sprung up around the squat, sturdy house with its dormer windows, front porch, and flagged walk. The Head's house was fixed, immutable, and beloved of generations of Woolies.

I looked out the big bay window behind the desk at the young figures scurrying from building to building and wondered at the violence of Louise's reaction to Margo Llewelyn's letter. I'd expected her to be puzzled but not indignant. Had she atrophied on the job? She answered this question by replacing the receiver and leaning forward, her palms on the desk.

"Mrs. Gamadge, I may sound like a flag-waving old girl, but Woolcott Academy is my whole life. It's been practically the only home I've ever known, and its reputation is everything to me. I don't want a notoriously disreputable alumna—"

"Louise," I had to interrupt. "How many disreputable alumnae do you suppose we have? You and I both know that every boarding school including this one has its share of messed-up children of messed-up parents."

"Of course I know that." She got up from behind her desk, then reached quickly for the tissue box. "But they don't all qualify for a feature spread in *People* magazine."

I suppressed a smile, half impatient, half sympathetic, as she poised her pink nose over a tissue and waited for the sneeze. Despite the misery of her cold, Louise Littleton was in every respect a very attractive woman with her dark hair, marvelous complexion, good figure, and grace of movement. She was elegant, appealing, and ever so slightly . . . priggish?

The door of her office opened, and her secretary came in. Celestra Riondo was fortyish, plump, efficient, and obviously mad about her boss. (She had ushered me into her office as if into a shrine.) As Louise sat down to sign the cluster of letters set before her, I asked Celestra how she had gotten her job. It seemed her family had fled from Cuba in the 1960s when she was ten years old and had been taken in by a wealthy friend in Miami.

The friend, an alumna of Woolcott Academy, had sent Celestra—who was very bright, Louise interjected—up to her alma mater where, despite only a smattering of English, she did well and quickly became fluent, distinguishing herself straight through to graduation.

"I'm very impressed," I said, smiling at her.

"God was good to me" was Celestra's reply, and when she'd left, I said I thought her remark oddly charming and devout.

Louise replied absently, her head in her hands, "Devout? Oh, yes, Celestra will save us all."

"Does she know that Margo Llewelyn was once Elaine Duffy, former Wooly?"

Louise looked up quickly. "Yes, and that's the problem. She idolizes her, prays for her every day, which is the reason I don't want Celestra here tomorrow if I decide to be here myself. She'd swoon with joy and and want"—another violent sneeze.

"—and want you to agree to anything."

"Exactly." Again the phone rang, and Louise reached for it. "Celestra had a breakdown last year. She's not completely stable."

I said, as she lifted the receiver, "I'm fairly stable, and I'm with Celestra. I want you to agree too."

Louise closed her eyes and entered into a discussion of a field trip to the Boston Aquarium. I got up and strolled about the room. It was larger than I remembered—yes, the folding doors that had divided the room had been removed, and the office was longer and sunnier. The door at the opposite end to the desk opened, I knew, onto stairs to the Head's living quarters. In the little foyer outside the office her secretary reigned.

I stood looking at the familiar bookcases, which were interspersed with shelves filled with ornaments and pictures. One photograph in particular held my eye. It was marked "Graduating Class, 1968." The girls were seated on the stone wall at the school's entrance. The first miniskirts revealed good legs and bad. One spectacular pair was jauntily crossed as Elaine Duffy, her arm linked with Louise Archer's, smiled her now famous smile.

Louise replaced the receiver as I turned and said, "Louise, forgive me, but I think you're overreacting. To begin with, we're not sure what she wants, and even if it's what we think, what do you really know about her that—"

"I know that she has three children." Louise got up and stood looking out the window. "They're all girls and quite young—the eldest is only twelve. Each child has a different father."

I stared. "How on earth do you know this?"

"Mrs. Gamadge," she turned, "surely you must realize that I've followed Duff's career in all its glory." She added grimly, "It's been easy enough to." She moved back to her desk and sat down again.

"Yes, I suppose so." I sat down myself, adding lamely, "I must admit, I don't keep up with . . ."

"Her first husband was Patrick Brimmer."

"Yes, even I remember that." It had been an anomalous, titillating union; the brainy, journalist/commentator and the goofily adorable movie star.

"Don't ask me who the other two undesirables were." Louise almost sniffed.

Rather daunting rectitude in one so relatively young, I thought.

"And of course her—shall we say—'extracurricular' activities are legendary. If—"

"Louise"—I leaned forward making my last pitch—"let her come and let her ask. The school year will be over in a few months, and you'll have till September to decide. By that time the picture may have changed, and she might—"

"I'll have my hands full enough in September." Louise smiled wryly. "Did you know we're admitting boys?"

I was surprised but not greatly so. "A wise move, I'm sure."

"A survival one, anyway. Enrollment is down, especially in the Lower School. But even that factor doesn't make me feel differently about this."

We were silent. She looked exhausted and ill as she stood up again restlessly.

"Mrs. Gamadge, I'm sure you think I'm callous or sanctimonious or something, but I just can't face it. Thank goodness tomorrow is Celestra's day off, and I intend to spend the day in bed."

"You certainly need to," I said quietly.

"So . . ." She came around the desk to me. "I'm asking a big, big favor. Will you please be here and see Duff and tell her no?"

"Louise!" broke from me. "No fair!"

That sent her, mercifully, into a fit of giggles. I was joining in, though rather indignantly, when the door flew open and Celestra stood before us in as dramatic a pose as her five-foot frame would allow.

"Mrs. Littleton! *Guess who is here!*"

3

We both knew instantly.

Louise gasped, "Typical!" and started for the other door. I stood up uncertainly, and Celestra cried, "But, Mrs. Littleton, it's—"

"I know who it is, Celestra. Mrs. Gamadge will see her." She was across the room, her hand on the doorknob.

"You *know*? But you *can't!* It's—"

The door behind Celestra flew open and a stunningly familiar figure burst in.

"Lou—if you run out on me I'll die!"

How to describe this woman's beauty and appeal? From her hair to her toes she was the same color, a lovely, slender, café-au-lait column. Yes, the famous face was blurred, but Margo Llewelyn radiated a charisma that Celestra and I stood drowning in as it swept across the room and reached Louise. She turned and stared. Margo took two steps, her arms outstretched. The next instant they were locked in a bear hug.

I dragged my eyes from them to look at Celestra; her expression was beatific.

Louise pulled away, gasping and laughing. "You said Thursday, you wretch!"

"I know. Then I panicked. I figured you'd split."

Louise, still laughing and coughing weakly, said, "It's all right, Celestra."

Celestra rolled her eyes and backed through the door exclaiming, "God is good!"

"He sure as hell is." Margo surveyed the coughing Louise. "Dammit, Lou, you sound awful. You should be in the infirmary."

"Oh, yes, a lot of good that would do with you barging in to make my day." Louise moved to her desk, her eyes on Margo. "Duff, this is Mrs. Gamadge, a good friend and an old Wooly."

"Mrs. Gamadge." She walked up to me, her hand out. "There was a pretty kid a few years behind Lou and me. Her name was Gamadge."

"My daughter, Paula. She'll be thrilled you remember her."

"Sure I do."

I reached for my handbag. "Well, I'll be off."

"Don't go!" It was a chorus of two, and they both laughed. Louise sat down at her desk reaching for the tissue box. She said, "Please stay, Mrs. Gamadge. This woman is trying to con me for something."

"Yes, please stay, Mrs. Gamadge, and help me con her." Margo threw her gorgeous handbag on the floor beside an armchair and sank down. A bit unwillingly, I sat. Margo gazed at her friend.

"Lou, you look knockout."

"Oh, come on. I'm a middle-aged school marm." Louise folded her arms on the desk and leaned forward smiling . . . and suddenly different. "But, you, Duff, so help me, you light up the room, as always."

Margo said, "It's black light now, pal."

16

"What's that?" I asked.

"The kind they use for certain effects. It brings out the glamour and hides the guts. Look, I was forty-five last week, and Lou gets it in May. On her it's just one year better for a terrific gal. On me . . . hey"—she got up quickly—"there used to be wine in that cabinet for visiting dignitaries. I snuck in once and tried some. Is there still?"

Louise nodded, and Margo dug in her handbag. A pillbox appeared, something was extracted and tossed into her mouth with one hand as she pulled open the door of the cabinet. Wine splashed into a glass, and she never stopped talking.

"My God, this room! I can't believe I'm here! Nothing—I mean *nothing* has changed except it looks bigger—sure, that's it—the doors are gone, and there's that antique globe and the bust of what's-his-name and—oh, no! Our class picture!" She seized it. "I didn't keep my copy—I hated them all except you. Will you look at who sits there with her big teeth? Her father was some wheel in Washington. What was her name? Fredrika Something?"

"*Please*, Duff, say it properly." Louise was grinning. "She'd only answer to Fred-er-ree-ka."

"Oh, yeah—Fred-er-ree-*ka-ka*." Louise and I exploded. "She was the bitch—oops, the *unpleasant girl*—who spread it around that I had no place to go during vacations—which was true, of course, unless I went home with you. Remember the time your grampa took us skiing in Quebec?"

"And my fourteen-year-old brother fell madly in love with you!"

They seemed to have forgotten my presence. I sat very still.

"Your folks were wonderful to me." Margo came back to her chair. "Not a bit snooty."

"Why should they be snooty? Really, Duff, you always did have such a persecution complex."

"You bet I did! Lou, my mother worked in the laundry of this place, and my father was unknown on land or sea. Hey"—Margo's voice changed—"you married Professor Littleton."

"Do you remember him?"

"Do I remember him! Every girl in the school including me had a crush on him."

"You know he died in Cambodia?"

"I know. And all I can say is what rotten luck, Lou. You poor kid, what absolutely rotten, lousy, stinking, frigging bad luck."

Louise said quietly, "Yes, that does rather describe how I felt at the time."

Could anyone else, I wondered, other than this lost friend, make Louise Littleton accept those violent, vulgar, infinitely consoling words?

"And since then"—Margo crossed her lovely legs—"you've been sort of, well, married to Woolcott Academy. And now you're the Head! It puts me a little in awe of you."

"So I've noticed," said Louise. We all laughed, and I was back in the picture. Louise leaned back in her chair. "Duff, what do you want?"

Margo seemed to go rigid. She hesitated, then said rapidly, "I want you to take my kids."

Louise started to flash me an I-told-you-so-look, but it stopped midway and jerked back to Margo. "*Kids?* Plural?"

"Yes, three. They're all girls. If you—"

"Duff." Louise stood up. "I won't say I'm surprised. I anticipated something of the sort, but not a request for your entire brood. Mrs. Gamadge and I were just discussing the matter, and I explained to her how impossible—"

"Don't say that!" Margo's eyes were closed, her voice hoarse. "Don't say it!"

"Dammit, Duff, listen to me!" Louise moved to the edge of her desk three feet from her friend. "I'm going to be very honest

and very cruel and selfish and holier-than-thou, but here it is."
She drew a breath, and I heard it wheeze in her throat. "Woolcott Academy is not a way station for a movie star and her
assorted husbands and boyfriends. I don't—"

"But there wouldn't—"

"—don't really want to contemplate Visiting Day when you all
descend separately or together, complete with photographers—"

"Their fathers would never come to see them." Margo stood
up. "And neither would I. Nobody would."

"But . . . but"—Louise looked dazed—"that's worse!" She
started to cough rackingly. I stood up and put my arm around the
vibrating shoulders.

Margo said, "I'm a pig."

"No, you're not," I said. "Why wouldn't anybody come see
them?"

"Because," she stood up, "I'll be in England, and nobody
would know where they are, not even their fathers."

Louise turned away, choking. I thought it was time for my
holding plan. I said,

"Miss Llewelyn—"

"Duff."

"Duff, we both know that Louise is in no shape to make a
decision now. By September when—"

"I'm not talking about September. I want them at Wooly
now—today."

"Today?" Louise whirled. "Are you crazy? Where are they?"

"In the car."

I began to laugh helplessly, Margo looked torn between
laughter and tears, and Louise simply stood speechless. Now
Margo stood up and leaned urgently forward, her hands on her
friend's shoulders.

"Lou, for God's sake, listen to me."

Louise turned her head away. "You'll catch my cold."

"The hell with your cold. Listen: I'm going to England to do a cameo bit in a movie, which I don't mind admitting I need. I can't drag the girls with me—even though I have complete custody of all three—it would be too brutal for them. I'll be gone about twelve weeks, maybe less, and I swear to you I'll walk back in here on or about Commencement Day. Is it still the first Sunday in June?" Her voice shook. "I want to leave my kids where I can have at least a *shred* of peace of mind. I want them together, and I want them with you. I'll play a full year's tuition for each one, and don't tell me Wooly doesn't need—"

"Duff, stop it!" Louise's voice was flat and angry.

Margo turned away, dug in her handbag, and made for the wine cabinet again.

Louise blew her nose and said quite calmly, "Do you remember a place in Vermont, a music camp run by nuns? Our Glee Club used to go up there on a bus to hear—"

"Sure I remember it. St. Cecelia House. I worked there summers."

Louise looked dazed. "I didn't know that."

"Nobody did. I made damn sure. All the rest of you were off at your summer houses or in Europe or wherever, and I was washing dishes in a camp in the boonies." She swallowed something else. "So what about the place?"

"It's a year-round school now." Louise moved back around her desk and opened a drawer. "Here's the address. A retired Sister there is a friend of mine. I'm sure they could use the money. If you—"

"No, no, *no!*" Margo shook her head violently. "I'll send the place a donation—the nuns were nice to me—but Lou, I want my girls with *you*. Three lousy months, that's all I'm asking—no, I'm begging. I'm begging you, Lou. *Three lousy months!*"

This was awful. I was grateful when the door opened and Celestra put in an apologetic face. "Mrs. Littleton, the man is here about the new gym suits. He says he only needs a few minutes—" She looked astonished as Louise almost fled past her out of the room.

Margo Llewelyn sat down again, her eyes closed, her fingers convulsively snapping and unsnapping the clasp of her handbag.

I walked to the window and saw three children draped over a car that bore a rental plate. They were watching the procession of students that crossed and recrossed the school grounds. I looked back at their mother and said, "Don't despair."

She broke into strangled sobs, covering her face with her hands. If it had been any other woman, I'd have instantly put my arms around her, but somehow I couldn't bring myself to embrace this ravaged goddess. I did the next best thing. I handed her the overworked box of tissues, took a pad and pencil from Louise's desk, and said, "Tell me the names and ages of your daughters and their fathers' names."

Margo looked up haggardly. "Why their fathers? I have complete custody—"

"Believe me, she'll have to know."

Margo drew a breath, mopped her face with a tissue, and said, "My baby is Christine. She's seven. Her father is Billy Venus; he's a singer. I don't suppose you ever—no. He nearly made it, and then he blew it. He's fourteen years younger than I am, and he's an alcoholic." She paused, looking into space, then went on. "The second oldest is Karen. She's ten. Her father is Frank Shugrue. He owns a nightclub in Beverly Hills which is actually a whorehouse, and he's dying of cirrhosis of the liver." She stood up. "The oldest is twelve. Her father is Patrick Brimmer."

"I'm familiar with that name, of course."

"Oh, sure. Big-shot newspaper writer. TV news and all that."

"And the child's name?"

"Louise."

It was so unexpected, so touching, that I looked up in surprise

21

and pleasure, but Margo had risen and was moving about rest-lessly. Now she turned suddenly.

"Mrs. Gamadge, what's your first name?"

"Clara."

"Clara." She walked over and stood before me. "I know you have children . . . maybe grandchildren?"

"Oh, yes."

"Then you have to understand. My girls are the only decent things in my life, and I want them here while I'm gone and nowhere else."

Actually, I didn't completely understand, and all I could do was look down at the pad to avoid looking at Margo, and say, "I'll admit the first two men on your list don't exactly inspire confidence, but Patrick Brimmer—"

"Don't waste any sympathy on Pat Brimmer." She turned away impatiently. "He gave up visitation rights to Louise years ago." She turned back as quickly and leaned down and touched my hand. "Oh, my dear, new friend Clara—can you persuade Louise?"

I said, trying to be practical and knowing practicality was out the window, "Well, today is out of the question. There's proce-dure, and Louise doesn't have the only say. There's the Board. And there are such things as grade transfers, health records—"

"I don't want to hear about that stuff!" Margo looked distract-edly about. "I just want it to happen *now*, and I'll pay anything. Absolutely anything. Wooly *must* be hard up for money."

"It is, but that's not a wise approach, Duff."

She gulped. "Sorry. I'm just so used to having it work." She stood still, mute and baffled.

I stood up, put the pad on Louise's desk, and said, trying to simplify the thing for myself, "What you really want is for Louise to board your daughters here for three months, scholastic and other considerations apart."

Margo nodded vehemently. "That's exactly what I want!"

A distant bell rang. I walked to the window again and looked out at her children. Now the tallest was stretched on the grass, and the other two sat beside her. Waiting. Waiting. Waiting. I felt Margo's eyes on me, and I said, without turning, "Why must it be today?"

"Because I'm on a British Airways flight at nine tonight."

I was turning from the window when a figure came into view. Louise walked down the steps of the house and stood perfectly still, looking at the children.

The imploring voice behind me said, "You'll root for me, won't you, Clara? Tell me you'll root for me."

It was not because Margo Llewelyn was calling me "Clara" and begging me—it was *not*. It was because I thought of my own granddaughters, safe in their cocoon of love, that I said, "Yes, I'll root for you." And sealed her fate.

4

A phone call to Paula enabled me to drive the children back to Dedham with me that afternoon.

Louise had simply said, "I'll speak to the Board" and didn't look at the check that Margo gave her with a kiss.

The girls showed little emotion at parting from their mother; evidently this was a familiar procedure, and I had a suspicion that in the course of hugs and whispers Margo had shortened the length of her projected absence. She spouted nonstop reassurance. She'd be back before they knew it, and guess *what?* For a few days before starting at Mummy's wonderful old school they were going to visit nice Mrs. Gamadge at her daughter's house where there were *cats!* And maybe other weekends would be spent there, and even when they stayed at school for the weekend—Mummy always did—there would be *such* interesting things to do! And how about *this*: during Easter vacation they might all go to New York to visit Mrs. Gamadge's other grandchildren and maybe see the Statue of Liberty! Wow! Were they *lucky*, and was Mrs. Littleton *super!*

Meanwhile nice Mrs. Gamadge was avoiding super Mrs. Littleton's eyes and praying that her own family would stand still for this scenario with all its possible complications. Also praying, but I guessed in unalloyed joy and thanksgiving, was a radiant Celestra, who stood throughout with hands clasped, lips moving silently.

During the drive back to Dedham, I was belatedly attacked by panic, and I alternated between attempts to quell it and attempts to assess the children.

There had been a comfortably familiar squabble between the two younger girls over who got the front seat. It was decided they would buckle in together, and Louise climbed in the back with a certain listlessness that saddened me, although she soon joined in the incessant jabber that ensued. I was asked what kind of car this was—a Ford, I said—and it was compared unfavorably with Mummy's Porsche. Was the school "hard," and what could they wear? I said I'd been told anything but jeans, and there was gloom. I tried to dispel this by talking about the cats. Then I announced that I wanted each of them to tell me what was her favorite subject in school, and during the rambling recitals that followed, I studied them as best I could.

The rearview mirror showed me Louise's round face and straight brown hair hanging rather limply on her shoulders. Just a tad phlegmatic and overweight? Beside me, and a tad *under*weight, Karen kicked wiry legs and wound and unwound the elastic on her ponytail. She had frizzy dark hair and wore glasses. None of them was a beauty, but Christine came closest with long light hair and the makings of a pretty profile. I wondered if Duff had looked like that at seven. She'd had all of these children in her thirties, I reflected. What had prompted those belated spurts of motherhood? No doubt the need for "someone to love me," so hard to come by in the course of an undisciplined life.

"—and she even *likes* to read. I think it's boring" were the words that brought me out of my reverie as we turned into Paula's driveway.

"Who likes to read?" I asked.

"Christine," replied Karen, "and she only just learned."

I looked with interest at this likes-to-read daughter of an alcoholic failed singer. I said, "Here we are."

Paula and Andy, though understandably dazed by their responsibility, behaved admirably and welcomed the visitors as if they were three kids from down the block who'd been invited to "sleep over." Janey and Andrea did a lot of staring at first—they were told the girls' mother was a friend of Gran's—then warmed up and took the two younger ones out to the backyard swings. Louise said she'd rather watch TV and sat down in the den. Paula and Andy and I had a consultation. Short of being directly asked for something by the girls, we decided to effect what Paula called her "benign neglect" policy.

I took the portable phone out to the kitchen where Andy was braising meat. Paula stood at the window with a view of the swings.

"It's so darned weird," she said, giggling. "It's like hiding hostages or something. I mean, what the heck are we supposed to do with them till we know if it's a deal at Wooly? They can't be left here alone. And I shouldn't take off from work, Mom."

"I'll stay here," I said.

"But you're going to Florida." Paula turned from the window. "And by the way, Sadd called."

I said, "The Wooly thing shouldn't take long if Louise pushes."

"Will she push, do you think?" Andy hovered over garlic-scented steam. "And will the powers-that-be agree? It's such a cuckoo arrangement."

"Private schools," I said, "are the natural home of cuckoo arrangements." I punched numbers on the phone. "What did Sadd want?"

"He wanted to know if you were sick of the weather up here and when you were arriving in Florida."

Three rings, four rings, I was resigned to hearing my son's voice telling me to leave a message, when the preadolescent croak of my grandson came on.

I said, "Hi, Hen, it's Gran."

"Hi, Gran." No thrill. "I'll get Mom."

I said over my shoulder to Paula, "Will you check on Louise? See if she'd like a potato chip or something? I hate to think of the poor kid sitting in there alone." I had a mental picture of Patrick Brimmer operating brilliantly somewhere on the globe. What on earth was I doing with his child?

My daughter-in-law's voice said, "Clara! Back in the Big Apple?"

"No, still up here at Paula's. Tina, let me ask you a question, and don't ask me why I'm asking."

"Sounds weird and just like you. Shoot."

"Could you put up three little girls for the Easter school vacation next month?"

A split second of hesitation. "We're thinking of Lake Placid and some skiing. But if—"

"I'll pay their way, of course," I said.

"That's not the problem, but—I mean—*three?* Whose kids are they?"

"Margo Llewelyn's."

Silence. Then Tina called offstage: "Henry! Pick up the phone. Your mother's gone nuts!"

———

But it happened.

Two days later, Margo Llewelyn's three daughters were accepted at Woolcott Academy, and Louise Littleton was given my assurance that if they were unhappy or proved intractable, Paula would take them and enter them in the public school with her own children. Paula was in turn assured that I would come back and play Nanny till their mother's return. This plan was to be relayed to Margo Llewelyn when she next contacted the school, but she did not, and had not, two weeks later. I was packing in my brownstone on East Sixty-third Street to go to Florida when the phone rang. It was Louise, and her voice was grim.

"Not a word," she said. "Absolutely nothing. No call, no letter, no message. An enormous box of chocolates for each child arrived last week. The cards read, 'I love you, Mummy.'"

"Where did the chocolates come from?" I asked.

"Mail ordered from Godiva."

"Do we assume she got on that plane and went to England?"

"We could assume she got on a plane and went to the moon. It makes me very uneasy. She was to let me know where she could be reached."

"She will," I said consolingly—and perhaps guiltily. "How are the kids doing?"

"Not too badly. Rather lost-seeming, but not stressed. We decided not to make undue scholastic demands on them, but already it's plain that the youngest is bright."

"She likes to read," I said.

"Yes, which is amazing considering her antecedents, but then genes do surface out of the distant past."

"What about your namesake's genes? Any signs of her distinguished papa's?"

"Not so far. And the middle one is hyper."

"Remember," I said, "Paula and I will take all or any if the situation gets hairy."

"I just wish Duff would get in touch. If nothing else, I'd like to thank her for the money. She was incredibly generous. But it's awful of her to just vanish from the scene."

"Leaving only a trail of chocolates," I said.

The trail progressed from chocolates to huge bins of popcorn to three expensive T-shirts from London. At least we knew Margo was there. But no return address was shown, and when I phoned Paula from Sadd's home on Santa Martina Island in Florida, I found out there had still been no letter, no call, no personal contact of any kind.

"But," said Paula, "Andy saw in a trade paper that she'd been seen in a nightspot in London. The word is she had a new boyfriend."

"How reassuring," I said.

"I had the girls here last weekend, and they brought her latest present—tapes of some English rock group. Andy went ape over them."

"How do they fare on other weekends?" I asked anxiously, my eyes on the blue-green waters of the Gulf of Mexico, the insane thought occurring to me that perhaps I should bring them here for a weekend.

"They do okay, I guess. Why shouldn't they? Stop agonizing, Mom."

"What about Easter? Is it still on for Lake Placid? Will Tina and Henry take them?"

"Yes. We're going too."

"Oh, Paula, that's wonderful! I'm so glad! I'll send you some money!"

That evening Sadd and I sat bathed in sunset and martinis on his patio. The gulf sparkled, gulls swooped, and egrets sidled up for tidbits.

"You're being rather a bore about this, Clara," Sadd said, as I voiced my hopes and fears for Margo Llewelyn's children for perhaps the fiftieth time.

"I know. I'll stop it." I tossed an olive into my mouth and another to a gull. "It's just that . . ."

"Just that you've gotten that poor Louise Littleton into this situation and you're in mortal dread that something will go wrong."

"Yes."

"Such as . . . ?" He regarded me as I gulped my drink. "That one of those kids might run away, or be abducted by her father, or some tabloid might discover—"

"Yes, all that. Now shut up, please. I promise not to mention them again."

"Clara, your weakness regarding children will be your undoing. You've allowed yourself to get involved with those waifs, who are probably completely uninteresting."

"That's hardly a reason not to pity them. And how do you know they're 'uninteresting'?"

"I don't, but it so often happens. Colorless children of dynamic parents. The kids are outclassed and outshone."

"All the more reason to, well, root for them." Margo's words. But she'd said "root for *me*," not them. Which had she meant?

"I suppose it's commendable," said Sadd, "but now that—"

"Now that I've stopped talking about it, may I have another cocktail?"

Sadd poured it, and we sat silently for a while in the glorious April evening, I longing for the first Sunday of June and all to be over.

"I must admit, however"—Sadd threw the last of the crackers on the grass, and wings beat around us—"that I envy your contact with Margo herself. I've always adored that woman. Is she as enchanting offscreen as on? Don't answer that!" He smiled ruefully.

"But she is. Even more so," I said. "And I believe she has a basic sense of honor. She told Lou, 'I swear to you I'll walk back in here on or about Commencement Day.'" She would. She would.

"But she's going downhill fast?" said Sadd.

"Oh, yes, fast. But she's still incredibly charismatic. You'd fall at her feet, Sadd."

He nodded dreamily. "What is there about certain women? I remember the first time I saw her in—"

"I thought we decided not to talk about Margo Llewelyn."

"I could talk about her forever. It's talking about her children that bores me."

I stayed on in that tropical paradise till May. It was a cold spring in New York, and I learned the routine of Florida visitors who daily check the weather in Boston or Buffalo, then settle snugly down for another few weeks.

"Am I invited for my usual visit to Cape Cod?" asked Sadd as he saw me off at the Sarasota airport.

"Of course. I have the cottage for June and July. Take your pick."

He heaved my carry-on to the conveyer. "I might just come up for commencement at Woolcott Academy. Catch a glimpse of the Woman I Love."

"I'm hoping she'll come before that." I must have sounded wistful, for he kissed me consolingly.

"You may get home to find she's been and gone and your worries are over."

If only that had been the case!

Back in my brownstone, I phoned son Henry at his law office in Brooklyn Heights.

"How did it go at Placid?" I asked.

"Went fine. No apparent trauma. Margo's kids had never skied so that was a newy for them. Hen volunteered to instruct them, and the oldest one developed a mad crush on him. We're wondering if her mom might sponsor a movie career for him. His talents aren't conspicuous along that line but—"

"Margo's not back?"

"I haven't heard. Oh, by the way, Louise Littleton presented Paula and me with a money order for two thousand dollars. It came from some English post office with a note that said Mummy hoped they'd have a nice Easter. It was sent to Louise, but she insisted on making it over to us."

"Good for her. But she still hasn't heard directly from Margo?"

"Apparently not."

Nor had Paula had any word. Of course, the thing for me to do was to call Louise, but I simply couldn't bring myself to. Only a few more weeks. I'd go up to Boston on Saturday, June first, and attend commencement next day. I owed that to Louise; and owing it, I prepared to do it with dread in my heart, for a sinister possibility had occurred to me, shaking my confidence in Margo. Was she buying her way with greater and greater largesse into an extended time period? Was she preparing us for her nonappearance? Was she assuring us that we wouldn't find her ungenerous should Commencement Day come and go and—no! I wouldn't think about it. But of course I had to.

If she doesn't appear, I thought, snapping shut my bag on that mild first morning of June, Louise cannot be expected to sponsor them further. I supposed I'd have to do something. What, in

God's name? Take them with me to the Cape? The thought was too appalling. My family had already extended themselves above and beyond. . . . And suppose—

The phone rang.

"Mrs. Gamadge! It's Louise! I *had* to call you!" The joy and relief in her voice floated across the wire and into my heart. "I got a cable from Duff! She's arriving this afternoon!"

"Louise! You're an angel for calling to tell me!" We were both practically weeping. "And I'm leaving for Boston in an hour—I'll come to commencement tomorrow and bring champagne!"

"Wonderful! See you then!"

What is there about relief that can jump-start one's morale? Only a minute before, I'd been dragging about throwing clothes in a bag. Now I whisked humming into the kitchen and made myself a Bloody Mary. I took it down to the tiny garden behind my house. A bit too chilly to sit, but just right for taking a rake and making first inroads on flower beds. Twenty minutes later I went back upstairs—eschewing the elevator because I felt so bouncy—ran a tub and sank into it holding the portable phone. My dependable taxi service said yes, I could be picked up for a 1:30 flight from La Guardia. I sank deeper in the tub trying to decide whether to eat lunch or wait for what Sadd calls "the cardboard colation" on the plane. The phone rang, and I reached for it lazily.

"Mom! It's me!"

"Paula—what's wrong?" I splashed erect.

"Oh, Mom . . ."

"*What?*"

"You haven't got your TV on?"

"No."

"I was afraid—I didn't want you to hear it at the airport"—a shaky intake of breath. "Margo Llewelyn's dead."

Blindly I reached for my robe. "Where? When?"

"Less than an hour ago. On the grounds of Wooly. She's been stabbed. Mom? Mom?"

"I'm here. Who found her?"

"Louise's secretary, the Cuban one. She was on her way to lunch. The body was under some bushes by the tennis courts. The media are going crazy. Oh, Mom, I wish I was with you!"

"You will be soon."

"I'll be at the airport early."

"Thanks, dear. Gotta run."

Run? When I could barely haul myself out of the bathroom and into my clothes? Margo Llewelyn stabbed and dead, Woolcott Academy jettisoned into the eager arms of the media, Louise's worst fears realized. She would never speak to me again. But even as I thought it, the phone rang and she was speaking to me.

"Mrs. Gamadge . . . come . . . please . . ."

5

"And—my God—commencement exercises are tomorrow! They'll have to cancel." Paula slowed for the policeman at the entrance.

"Commencement." That civilized word rang strangely in this scene of hectic disarray. The grounds of Woolcott Academy swarmed with police and press. It was *People* Magazine Heaven. I winced, remembering Louise's words. On the road, held at bay but milling and peering, was a crowd that Paula had inched the car through.

"Officer, Mrs. Littleton is expecting us," she said to the policeman.

"Name?"

"Gamadge."

"Go ahead. That stone house there."

We pulled forward. No sign of a student anywhere, but windows bristled with faces. I was sure that rigidly controlled conditions prevailed within the school.

Between the driveway and the road, the tennis courts with

their surrounding bushes were cordoned off and dense with police.

"I won't go in and add to the confusion." Paula slowed before the Head's house, and a young, redheaded policeman came down the steps. "Call me if you change your mind and want to come home."

"I'll stay here. Or in the town. Or someplace."

The policeman said, "Mrs. Gamadge?"

"Yes. Will you take my bag, please?"

"Sure."

He got it and went up the steps. Paula kissed me and said, "You know I'll take her kids if need be—for a while."

But I shook my head. "No more of that. It's different now."

I got out of the car, and she drove away. It was chilly, and I pulled my raincoat around my shoulders. A couple of persons with writing pads started to edge toward me. I was somebody; the police had expected me. I hurried into the house, and the young man closed the door behind us.

Celestra's desk. He pointed to it and said, "That poor soul found the body. I know her slightly. She goes to my church."

"Where is she?"

"Collapsed. There's a little clinic in one of the school buildings where she boards. She's there."

The phone on the desk rang. "They got it turned off in there," he said, nodding toward the office. "This is maybe the fiftieth time." Wearily, he intoned, "Woolcott Academy . . . She can't come to the phone. . . . Yes, commencement will be held tomorrow as scheduled."

Good for Louise!

The office door opened, and elderly, keen-eyed man with thinning white hair—Lionel Barrymore to a T—said, "Clara!"

Who was he? How did he know me? I hadn't time to ask before Louise was rushing at me, and he and I were getting her back into the office, and she was weeping, and he was saying she hadn't done that until this minute. I took a flask of brandy from my handbag—preparedness is all—and said, "Drink a little of this."

I held it to her white lips, and she sipped and sputtered and shuddered. Lionel Barrymore said, as I plied her again, "Why didn't I think of that?" He went to the door and put his head out.

"It's Jim, isn't it?"

"Yes, sir," from the redhead.

"Mrs. Littleton has talked to the police, and she's not to see another soul till I say so. As her lawyer, I can make that stick."

"Yes, sir."

"How long can you stay, Jim?"

"Until my boss pulls me off."

"Let me know if he does. We'll get somebody from the school to take your place."

He closed the door, and I thought of poor Celestra and how she'd have loved the job of manning the defenses. Then he turned.

"Clara, I'm Harry Parr. My sister Rose was—"

"In my class, of course! Your parents were wonderful. They took us to plays and things." I held out my hand, and for a second or two we existed in a safe old world.

He said, "Louise tells me you've been involved in this sort of thing before."

"Never in anything with such a high profile. Thank God you're here, Harry."

"Mr. Parr was wonderful." Louise was clinging to my hand. "He heard the news on his car radio and came right over. I couldn't believe it. He got here while they were still—while Duff was still—"

"Shush," I said and pulled a chair beside her. "Where are the children?"

"Smartest thing she ever did." Harry sat down behind Louise's desk. "She broke the news to the poor little things and put them on a plane to Vermont."

"Vermont?" For a second or two I was puzzled. "Oh . . . St. Cecelia House?" Louise nodded. "Who went with them?"

"Mrs. Manetti and her husband. She's our music teacher."

"Louise, that was inspired."

"I had to do something." She looked at me distractedly. "They couldn't be left here. They'd have been mincemeat." She shivered. "Already reporters were climbing up fire escapes to try and get pictures of them. As soon as it became known why Margo Llewelyn was on these grounds . . ."

"It really hit the fan," said Harry.

"I called Sister Beranice. She's my friend there." Louise started to get up, but I pushed her gently back onto the chair. "And she said of course send them till this had 'blown over.' *Blown over.* As if it ever will."

"Of course it will," said Harry briskly. "And you're a good sport to go through with commencement tomorrow. I appreciate having my granddaughter graduate properly. After all, she's a third-generation Wooly."

Louise smiled wanly. "Mr. Parr's daughter, Ann, was in my class and—and Duff's."

"Duff." Harry picked up a letter opener and stared at it. "I've adored that woman since the first time she kissed me. She was probably sixteen. I'd come over here from my office on my daughter's birthday to take her to lunch. She asked if she could bring a few friends along. Among them was Louise Archer and a vision they called 'Duff.' When I brought them back to school, the girls all thanked me and shook hands like perfect ladies. All except Duff. She kissed me."

There it was. Always—probably from birth—unforgettable. Harry threw down the letter opener and stood up. "Well, to work. First, a couple of important questions."

38

"Dear God, yes." Louise closed her eyes. "Who could have done this?"

"Actually, that wasn't going to be one of them, for now anyway." He came around to the front of the desk and leaned against it. "But who did it? Plenty of candidates, I'd say. Her life was a shambles. Take, for instance, her gang of husbands. Her slew of lovers. At least one of them must have hated her. Right now my question is—"

The door opened, and Jim leaned in. "Can I speak to you, sir?"

Harry hesitated, then went out closing the door behind him. Louise and I looked at each other.

I said, "Can you forgive me?"

"What for?" She slumped back in the chair. "I'd probably have taken the children anyway. She always got her way." Then, looking away, "Is she—I mean—do you know where . . . ?"

"They took her to the Norwood Hospital, Paula said. It's the nearest."

"What happens next?"

"The medical examiner will order an autopsy. It's the law."

"They told me . . . the knife was still in her back."

"Yes."

I got up, realizing I was still clutching my raincoat around me, and threw it on a chair. "Louise, who has contacted you? Her lawyer? Her agent? Her—"

"Just her agent. Ghastly sounding person. He wants the body sent back to California to some place where they dress it up and prop it up and people can walk by and look at it."

"Oh, God, yes. One of those upholstered morgues. Awful."

We both started to shake a little, and I produced the flask again but Louise said no, she'd be sick, so I took a swig myself and said, "Well, nobody can do anything about anything without her lawyer. I wonder why you haven't heard from him—or her."

"Out of the country maybe?"

"Even so. The news is all over the world by now. I remember sitting in the Zurich airport years ago looking at a newsstand with headlines screaming JUDY GARLAND EST MORTE!"

The door opened, and Harry came back. He took up exactly where he'd left off. "Now my question is this, Louise: Were you expecting Margo Llewelyn here today?"

"Yes, I had a cable from her this morning. Celestra took it over the phone and wrote it down. I think it's there on my desk."

"When you called that school in Vermont, did you ask the Sister not to mention who the children are?"

"Yes. And of course their names bear no relation to Margo Llewelyn's."

"True. I have a particular reason for asking you all this."

Harry started to walk around the room, which I realized had grown rather dark. Had it begun to rain? I pulled the curtain across the window, snapped on the desk light, and seated myself there. Harry and I moved; Louise appeared immobilized. Now Harry faced us.

"First I have to tell you something which will come as a bit of a shock." He seemed to be choosing each word carefully. "Has it occurred to you . . . to wonder . . . why you haven't heard from Margo Llewelyn's lawyer? Well, you have. It's me."

Shock? It was more like a bewildering blast. Louise and I simply looked at him, and he went on, beginning to walk again.

"Of course, it won't be me for long—I can't represent you both—but before I turn you over to someone I can trust—"

Louise gasped, "Mr. Parr—how?—why—"

"Harry, what *is* this?" I said.

"I know, I know. I'll explain." He looked at me imploringly and sat down beside Louise. "Just give me this minute to sneak something in while I can. Time is desperately important now. Louise, the fathers of those kids will be descending on you very shortly, and believe me, they're quite a collection."

She nodded mutely.

"At least two of them will smell money, and every one of them will want to know where his daughter is."

"Of course. And I'll tell them. They can go get—"

"I wouldn't," I said.

"Wouldn't what?"

"Tell them where the girls are," said Harry.

"Not tell them!" Louise looked shocked. "But I must. Whether we like it or not, they are the children's fathers, and if—"

"Louise," I said, and Harry was nodding vigorously, "those three men, especially Patrick Brimmer, are in the spotlight right now. Unless they have alibis, probably all three are suspects. If they take off for Vermont, the press will be after them, and all your efforts to protect the girls will go down the drain."

Louise looked bewildered and doubtful. "But . . . what shall I tell them?"

"Tell them," I said, looking at Harry for approbation, "that their daughters are in a safe place where they won't be photographed or questioned or harassed, and . . . and . . . ," I was running out and Harry finished for me,

". . . and that you will use your own best judgment as to when they may be fetched."

He was sitting forward in his chair seeming to want to say more.

I had a sudden qualm. "Can she really afford to be so cavalier, Harry?"

"Yes, she can."

My mind raced. "Then . . . none of these men will be allowed the guardianship of his child?"

"None. They gave up their rights. Just as well. Two are unfit, and the third apparently doesn't want it. The guardianships have gone elsewhere, and *that's* going to be a can of worms." He stood up. "So, be firm about leaving the children where they are for the time being." He looked thoughtful. "Patrick Brimmer might even thank you."

Louise smiled halfheartedly. "Patrick Brimmer. I read his column. I've often thought I'd like to meet him."

"You will. Tonight. He's at the Woolcott Inn." We both stood and stared. "That was the message Jim just gave me. Brimmer lives in Connecticut and drove up. Didn't I tell you time was of the essence? And do you feel like betting? We'll hear from the other two before morning. Clara"—he looked at me but gestured toward Louise—"get this woman upstairs and into a warm shower."

I stood up but said sternly, "Harry, you still haven't told us—"

"Why and how I'm Margo Llewelyn's lawyer." He looked at his watch. "Five o'clock. Go upstairs both of you and get comfortable. I'm going out to get some beer and then over to the dining hall for a bite. I'll have some supper sent over to you, then I'll join you back here in an hour, ready to confess all—word of honor."

He was herding us toward the door to the stairs, and I was torn between exhaustion, hunger, and a certain foreboding. Louise appeared more trancelike than torn. As we reached the door, the phone on her desk rang shrilly and we all jumped. Harry said, hurrying to it, "I told Jim to let this call come through." Louise and I stood still and listened.

Squawking preliminaries, then Harry said, "Mr. Shugrue, there's no need to get worked up. . . . Thank you. Yes, your daughter—*please*, Mr. Shugrue. . . . Of course Mrs. Littleton will see you. Where are you? The Holiday? That's ten minutes from here. Take a left as you leave the motel, and Woolcott Academy is a few miles down on Route 40. Shall we say eight o'clock? I'm sorry, it's out of the question before that. . . . Your attitude is rather unfortunate, Mr. Shugrue. As Margo Llewelyn's lawyer I can assure you . . . eight o'clock then. Give the policeman at the entrance your name, and he will tell you where to come."

Harry hung up. "I nearly said 'where to *go*.' That was Husband Number Two. Delightful guy." His face was somber. "How could Duff have gone from Brimmer to that . . ."

Louise said faintly, "Must I see them both tonight?"

"Both and tonight. Get it over with. They'll want to know where your lawyer is, so let's fake it and say he's on his way and you're representing him, Clara."

I said, "Why fake it? My son and his wife are both lawyers. Shall we ask them to take you on, Louise?"

She nodded and tried to say something. Harry looked grateful. "That's the only good news I've heard today. Now, off with the pair of you."

As we started up the stairs, the phone rang again. Louise gagged.

"I don't want to listen."

"Neither do I." The thing was assuming antic proportions. We reached the top of the stairs, and Louise said dully, "I should go over and see poor Celestra."

"Haven't you yet?"

"Only when she rushed into the office screaming something about Margot Llewelyn—and passed out."

"She may still be sedated. I'll go with you later, or tomorrow."

"Okay." She opened a door. "You're in this room, Mrs.— Clara." She put her arms around me. "How can I ever thank you for coming?"

"By going straight in and taking that warm shower."

She moved down the narrow hall with its lovely, worn Persian runner and went into a room. I waited till I heard the shower going and then went back down the stairs. Harry was just setting down the phone receiver. He turned and saw me and came to the door.

"That was the Third Man. He just landed in Boston from the West Coast. Have you ever tried giving driving directions to a drunk? I tried to persuade him to—"

"Harry, I have two questions: the first is about the funeral. Her agent has already been on the phone to Louise wanting—"

"No funeral. Cremation, and I'm to take the ashes. Her will is specific about it."

"Thank God. I assume she'll be kept in the hospital morgue until after the autopsy?"

"Yes. No media allowed, and identification required of anyone wanting admission. Cremation following the inquest."

I sat down on the steps; I might need to. "Now for my second question: you said the guardianship of the children has gone 'elsewhere.' By 'elsewhere,' do you mean what I think you do?"

He nodded and leaned against the door looking distressed. "I hadn't the heart to hit her with it on top of everything else. But I'll have to tonight. I dread it more than anything."

I tried to focus. "But doesn't the person—the guardian have to—I mean, she wasn't consulted."

"True. And for that reason she can turn it down. God knows where the guardianships would go, of course . . ."

He walked back across the office and stood at the desk fiddling with something. I stood up and steadied myself on the newel.

"Why on earth didn't you—"

"I know . . . tell Louise at the time. I should have. But in February when Duff asked me"—he came halfway back and stood still. "Can I give you all my alibis and excuses later when I have to break it to Louise?"

I looked at Harry thinking, Duff, you really socked it to your old friend, didn't you? I said, "Would you like me to tell her?"

"Oh, Clara, would you?"

6

Well, that nearly did it for Louise.

She began to laugh and cry at the same time, sitting on her bed in a pretty yellow terry robe, drying her hair with a towel and gasping that she didn't believe it and wouldn't do it. I made no comment, just refilled her glass with some iced tea that I found in her little refrigerator, and stood looking out the window at the beginning of long shadows in her garden; the Head's house had always had beautiful flower beds. From this window the school's entrance was just visible, and the crowd appeared to have thinned. My watch said 6:15.

Several times footsteps had pattered up the stairs, and bright-eyed girls had said the officer at the door said they could come up with this or that message. Mrs. Prothero, the assistant principal, wanted Mrs. Littleton to know that everything was under control, she wasn't to worry, and what a blessing that she had a friend staying with her. Mr. Brady, the custodian, assured her that all buildings were secured and that Mr. Parr had arranged for shifts of police to take Jim's place when he left. Mrs. Antoole, the school nurse, sent a message saying that Celestra was better and might be able to resume her duties in a day or two—and by the way, it made her especially happy to know that she had taught Margo Llewelyn's children the Lord's Prayer and she hoped it was a consolation to them now. Bishop and Mrs. Staples thought that dear Louise was very courageous to continue with commencement despite everything, and they'd be there to preside as usual. Mrs. Owens, the chemistry teacher, sent word that she was establishing herself at Celestra's desk to take calls, and Hilda Larkin, the coach, sent fruit.

Everybody wanted to know "if there's anything I can do," that universally kind and oddly ineffectual question.

I turned from the window. "Louise, don't make any decision on this matter right now."

"Sorry—it's made. I won't do it."

She walked into the bathroom and plugged in a hair dryer. No use trying to talk over that, and probably just as well. Mind your own business, Clara. You twisted her arm once before, and the roof has fallen in. I waited for the dryer to stop, then said, "I agree with the bishop and Harry. You're a good sport to go through with tomorrow."

"I'll be darned if I'll let all this spoil things for the graduates." She stopped in the act of winding the dryer cord and frowned. "I hope Celestra finished the diplomas. Her lettering is beautiful." She stared at herself in the mirror. "Look at the gray." I saw none. Her short, fluffy dark hair was charming.

Another knock. A plump, blond adolescent stood at the door with a covered tray. Louise said, "Thank you, Tricia. Put it over there. This is my friend, Mrs. Gamadge."

We exchanged smiles, and Tricia said, "Mr. Parr said he's sending over a bottle of wine. Mrs. Owens will bring it up."

"That will be nice."

Tricia said, "Did Louise and Karen and Christine have to leave school?"

"Yes. It seemed best."

"I know it's rotten for them, but it's kind of exciting, isn't it? Kind of like something on TV."

We stared at this creature from another planet, and Louise said, "Yes, well, thank you, Tricia." The girl departed, and Louise turned to me. "Clara, you haven't so much as sat down. Please eat something." She lifted a corner of the tray cover. "I'm not sure I can."

"Of course you can . . . and should." I picked up half a sandwich. "But first I'm going down for that wine and to make a call to my son. You're sure you want Henry and Tina to represent you?"

"Is that his name? Is he Junior? And his wife is a lawyer too?"

"Yes."

"Certainly I want them. It's a fabulous break." She walked to a closet, unbelting her robe. "I remember your husband so well. He used to talk to us silly girls about rare books as if any of us knew anything about anything. What a dear man."

"Louise," I said, "wear something pretty."

She looked over her shoulder in surprise. "Why?"

"I want you to impress these characters."

"Why should I impress them? I'll never see them again."

"That's attractive." I walked over to her and pulled from the closet a pale green challis print with a scoop neck. "Becoming too, I'll bet. Wear it."

I turned to look at her and was astonished to see tears in her eyes. "Is this what mothers do? I love it. No one ever said to me 'wear this' or 'wear that.' I never knew my mother."

"Neither did I, but a dear aunt did for her. Trust Aunt Clara. Wear this."

47

I went out and down the stairs feeling a surge of compassion for this woman. How vulnerable she was despite her thorough professionalism. Was it fair to her to hope she might change her mind? I tried to envision Margo Llewelyn's children adrift on the Hollywood seas and decided yes, dammit, it was fair to hope.

I crossed the office and opened the other door. A nice-looking young black woman holding a bottle of wine and a corkscrew was getting up from behind Celestra's desk. She said, "Mrs. Gamadge? I was just going to bring this up."

"Thank you, Mrs. Owens. Will you do that? And be sure Mrs. Littleton has some. May I tie up your phone for a few minutes?"

"Please do. That's the best thing that could happen to it."

She went out, and I punched my son's number in Brooklyn. The phone rang three times. I looked at my watch. Between office and home? No, this was Saturday. One more ring, and the message started. "You have reached"—the receiver was snatched off, and my daughter-in-law's out-of-breath voice said, "Made it! Hello."

"Tina."

"Clara—my God! We've been trying to reach you, and we couldn't get through! Paula said she delivered you to Wooly. Are you okay? Henry! Pick up!"

My son's voice said, "This is one for the books, Mom."

"It isn't one for my book. I'm way out of my depth."

"What do you mean?"

"There's no way I could possibly find out who killed Margo Llewelyn, and I have no wish to try. I'm concerned for just one thing, her children. Margo has left the guardianship of all three to Louise—"

"Wow!" from Tina.

"And she's going to need a lawyer—one or both of you, I hope."

A pause, then Henry said, "You mean to say she doesn't *have* a lawyer?"

"Well, the school has one, but he's also"—no, it was too weird to explain over the phone. "Could you possibly—I mean—tomorrow's Sunday—er—fly up? I'll ask Paula to meet you."

Another pause, then Tina said, "Ball game."

"What?"

Henry said, "Hen has a game tomorrow. He's pitching. One of us ought to be there. I'll volunteer for Tina. Will you go up, hon?"

"Okay."

I said, "Tina, I feel like a rat." This was a baseball family. "I bet you were at practice this afternoon."

"Yes, just got in. I'm glad we didn't miss your call. Shall I let Paula know what plane?"

"Please, dear. And will you put Hen on for a minute? I want to tell him I'm sorry about you missing the game."

But my grandson was another Tricia. "Wow, Gran! You might even get on TV with this one! Far out!"

"But Mr. Parr, you should have told me back then!"

It was half past seven, we were sitting in the office, and Margo Llewelyn's "gang of husbands" was expected in half an hour. Louise looked lovely in the green challis; I was trying to look dignified in what, I imagined, a "lawyer's representative" might wear, and poor Harry was rumpled, apologetic, and pacing. As she had sat down, Louise stated rather peremptorily that she declined the guardianship of the children.

"My dear girl, of course I should have told you then. Let me explain—or maybe just . . . rationalize."

He sat down at her desk. Louise and I were on two other

chairs, the lamp on the table between us the only light in the room. Judging from sounds on the window, it was raining hard. Harry glanced at his watch, then folded his hands on the desk and looked down at them, not at us.

"It was last winter. I got a call from Margo Llewelyn asking if she could come to me." He paused, and I thought how odd and rather touching; not "she asked if she could come see me" or "come to my office" but "come to me." Almost a lover's phrasing. Duff could unconsciously make a man think of an appointment as a rendezvous.

"She said she'd inquired who the school lawyer was and that she remembered my name, even that she remembered me, but that I doubt." But oh, how lovely for Harry to hear her say it. "Well, she came. She told me she was going to England to make a movie and that she hoped to leave the children with you. She wanted to make a new will with everything in trust for the girls. Each trust is enormous, I might add, which is probably one of the reasons"—he looked at his watch again—"that we're expecting our visitors. Then she said she wanted to name you as their guardian."

Harry pushed his chair back a little, almost as if he felt our two pairs of eyes riveted on him uncomfortably.

"She assured me that she had total custody of all three and that I could check this for myself, which I did. Believe me, I did some very thorough checking. The third husband is some singer I'm supposed to have heard of but haven't, and is an alcoholic, the second one owns a highly suspect "nightclub" in Glendale and has a liver disease, and the third, Patrick Brimmer, hasn't asked to see his daughter in three years. That surprised me. I like his work and wouldn't have thought . . . In any any event"—Harry looked straight at Louise—"I said we would have to ask your permission to name you guardian. Well, Duff was adamant, even . . . even imploring." Duff at her best! "She reminded me that she would only be gone a few months and that the guardian-ship was a far-fetched eventuality, only effective in the event of her . . . death."

Harry's last words hung there, and we were silent. The phone on the desk rang, and he lifted the receiver. He said, "Thank you, Mrs. Owens. Please ask him to wait just one moment."

He stood up. "Well, I went along with her. It was probably unethical, but I did." He came around the desk and stood before us. "And now I'm going to be even more unethical and tell you something you shouldn't know till the will is read. Duff has left Woolcott Academy a very generous bequest."

"Harry!" I beamed on him. "That's downright bribery, and I'm proud of you!"

He smiled, but Louise only shook her head in a dazed way and looked at the door with dread. She said, "Which one of them is it?"

"Patrick Brimmer."

Harry went to the door, and Louise stood up nervously as he opened it. He said, "Please come in, Mr. Brimmer. I'm Harry Parr, Margo Llewelyn's lawyer."

The man's long, lined face, deep-set eyes, and graying hair were familiar to all of us, but I hadn't expected him to be so tall.

"I hope I'm not being precipitous," he said.

"Not at all. This is Mrs. Littleton, Head of Woolcott Academy, and her friend Mrs. Gamadge."

Louise held out her hand, and Brimmer took it with what I interpreted as a surprised look, Mrs. Gamadge probably being more along the line of what he had expected. Harry pulled forward another chair.

"Mrs. Gamadge is representing her daughter-in-law, who is Mrs. Littleton's lawyer. She's on her way up from New York. The suddenness of this whole ghastly thing—"

A loud male voice and Mrs. Owens's protesting one came to us

51

through the door, then it was pushed open by a short, flashily dressed man with a round, blotched face. Mrs. Owens's indignant one looked over his shoulder. She said, "This is Mr. Shugrue."

Harry advanced and said politely, "Please come in and sit down, Mr. Shugrue. I'm Harry Parr, Margo Llewelyn's—"

"I got no time to sit down or nothin'. I just came to pick up my kid."

7

It would be hard to say which was more offensive, his manner or his tone. The man was appalling, almost cartoonlike. We reacted with embarrassment, that is Louise and I did, sitting down and looking at each other in disbelief. Brimmer simply walked to the bookcase, pulled out a volume, and opened it, his back to us.

Harry recovered first. He said quietly, "There's procedure here, Mr. Shugrue. I strongly advise you to take a chair." Shugrue planted his feet and stood still. "I was about to introduce you to Mrs. Littleton, Head of Woolcott Academy"—Louise looked in Shugrue's general direction and nodded slightly—"and the lady who represents her lawyer, Mrs. Gamadge." My nod was even slighter. "Perhaps you know Patrick Brimmer."

"No, but I heard of him." Shugrue looked resentfully at Brimmer's back. Then he took a step toward Louise. "I hope you got my daughter packed."

Louise looked up at him with admirable calm. "Your daughter isn't here, Mr. Shugrue."

His eyes, sick and filmy, widened.

I said, I hope as calmly, "All three of Margo Llewelyn's children have been sent to a safe place to save them from being exploited."

He looked blank. "What's ex—what's that mean?"

"Used." Brimmer half-turned. "One of the worst things that can happen to a child, and I personally thank Mrs. Littleton."

"Well, I don't." Shugrue stared at Louise. "I think it was very high-handed, and you should of asked us first." He shifted his feet. "Look, Mrs.—er—Little . . . I don't mean to insult you or nothin', but if you'll kindly tell me where Karen is I'll go get her. If you're owed any money, I'm sure there's a trust fund for the kids that'll take care of you."

The phone rang, and Harry said, "Yes . . . ? Ask Mr. Venus to come in." The door opened, and Mrs. Owens, looking impressed, said, "Billy Venus."

My children told me later that I should have recognized the name and face of this rock star of the 1980s, but so scant is my knowledge of the field that neither registered. I saw only a frail young man, probably in his thirties, with matted blond hair and a nervous smile. With one hand he clutched a soiled yellow slicker around him, and with the other he steadied himself on a chair near the door. Mrs. Owens said, "I could take that wet coat," but he shook his head and clutched it tighter and she went out.

Shugrue said, "For Chrissake, Billy, how'd you ever get here in one piece?"

Harry said, "Mr. Venus, I'm Harry Parr, Margo Llewelyn's lawyer."

Brimmer said, his eyes on his book, "So the gang's all here."

Louise and I said nothing. We were speechless.

It was the utter incongruity of the thing. How had Duff managed to assemble such a bizarre triumvirate and land them here in this room for her friend to sort out? In the brief but baffled silence that followed, rain could be heard beating on the window as if it would never stop. I thought guiltily of poor Tina arriving at the Boston airport tomorrow and poor Paula struggling through traffic to meet her. Clara, you have a nerve.

"And I think it only decent for us to keep in mind," Harry was saying, "that a woman who figured largely in the lives of all of us is lying dead in a hospital two miles from here. I'd appreciate it if you gentleman would give me your attention."

Harry picked up his briefcase and set it beside him as he sat down at the desk. None of the three men had moved. Now it was only Billy Venus who pulled forward the chair he'd supported himself on, and slid onto it. Shugrue stood stubbornly still, looking haggard and exhausted, and Patrick Brimmer never moved or took his eyes from his book. I got the impression that he couldn't bear to look around.

A strained silence ensued, during which Harry studied some papers on the desk before him, humming gently. You old faker, I thought—good for you. You're dying inside, thinking of lovely Duff. How could she have become involved with these characters? Billy suddenly started talking.

"I seen you on TV," he said, clear as a bell, gazing at Brimmer, "Margo used to talk about you sometimes. I remember once she said, 'In my career, I started at the bottom and worked my way *up*, but in my marriages, I started at the top with Patrick and worked my way *down* to you, Billy.' " He laughed and hiccuped.

We were motionless except for Harry, who zipped his briefcase.

Then Shugrue swayed and got himself to the chair by the desk. He sat down and said, "Do they know who killed her?"

"Not yet, I believe." Harry gathered his papers together, "and I feel I should remind you gentlemen that the police will question you as to your whereabouts this afternoon. You undoubtedly know that because—"

"I don't 'undoubtedly know' nothin'." Shugrue's voice was harsh. "Except that I was in the Marriott in New York and they can't pin a thing on me." He leaned slightly toward Louise. "And maybe Mrs.—er—Little should get that question too."

Time for Mrs.—er—Little's lawyer's rep to speak up. I said, "She's already been asked that question by the police, Mr. Shugrue. By the way, I understand you operate a business on the West Coast."

"So?"

"So what brought you to New York this morning—before Margo Llewelyn was killed?" I'd watched the news while Louise was dressing. "Not," I hastened to add, "that I'm interrogating you—I haven't the right—but just to remind you that you will be asked that question."

"I'm in New York to see a specialist!" said Shugrue violently.

Brimmer said, turning a page of his book, "I expect to be rather hard put for an alibi. I might very well have been here on the school grounds this afternoon, instead of in my home in Greenwich, Connecticut, where I was correcting proofs."

Billy said, "Jeez, I never thought they'd think I killed Margo. I had nothing against her really, except when she wouldn't let me see Christine."

"Or wouldn't let you see some money, Billy," said Shugrue.

"What do you mean by that?" Billy flared.

"Come on! You started borrowing off Margo while I was still married to her."

"And I started paying her back while *I* was still married to her!"

"Started and stopped."

"How would you know?" Billy struggled to his feet, weakly furious.

Was this sordid exchange actually taking place in this room? Louise looked imploringly at Harry, but he shook his head and let it go on.

"He knows, Mr. Venus"—Brimmer closed his book and turned—"because he had also stopped paying Margo what he owed her and for exactly the same reason." He looked directly at Louise. "I'm afraid, Mrs. Littleton, that we're a very scurvy trio. And I'm probably the worst of the bunch, because I never owed Margo Llewelyn a cent, but I gave her what she wanted anyway."

Louise said, unexpectedly, "Your daughter."

"My daughter. I told myself it was better for the child not to be subjected to her mother's tantrums every time a visit was proposed, so I stayed away."

"We all stayed away." Shugrue's hands twitched. " 'Keep away from your kid,' she said, 'and you don't have to pay me what you owe me.' Crazy possessive about those kids."

"But last week," Billy said, sinking dejectedly onto his chair again, "comes her letter."

"Shut up, Billy," said Shugrue quickly.

"Why? I didn't kill her, and I got an alibi to prove it."

"So do I, so do I." Shugrue's voice was thick.

"Beat this: I was sitting at my agent's pool with a bunch of people at nine o'clock this morning California time. Noon here. Margo was just getting it."

"And I checked into the Marriott in New York this morning for a medical appointment I should be at right now, and here's the card that proves it!"

Our eyes had been going back and forth between the two as at a tennis match. Shugrue pulled out his wallet with trembling fingers and threw a card on the desk before Harry. Then he glared around. "Why pick on us just because we were married to her once? We all know she slept with a million other guys. I can give you—"

"Mr. Venus," said Harry, "you said something about a letter?"

"Yeah, she wrote that she needed money and she was going to call in all her chips when she got back from England. Hell, I didn't even know she was *in* England."

"Neither did I!" Shugrue reached over to retrieve his card, which Harry hadn't touched. "And that's just what I mean! Look . . . the truth is Margo grabbed the kids a long time ago, and that was that. I haven't seen her—or my daughter—in a coupla years."

"Me neither," said Billy.

A pause, then Harry said, "What about you, Mr. Brimmer?" and all eyes went over the net in that direction. "When did you last see Margo Llewelyn?"

Brimmer slid his book back into its place on the shelf and spoke over his shoulder. "I saw her about an hour ago. Her body, that is. In the hospital morgue."

Stunned silence. Louise half rose, then sat down again. Nobody else moved.

Then Billy said with a gulp. "You . . . *went* there?"

"Yes."

"You *looked* at her?"

"Yes." Brimmer, his hands in his pockets, faced us with an expression of calm indifference. It was obvious he wasn't going to elaborate further. Harry was looking at him with what I took to be respect, and I'm sure Louise was envisioning, as I was, that sheeted figure. . . .

We were brought back to grubbiness by Shugrue standing up and saying, "I don't want to hear nothin' about it—how she looked or *nothin'!*" He reached Louise in a stride. "Lady, just tell me where my daughter is, and I'm out of here."

Louise looked at him and suddenly became another woman. She stood up and faced him so squarely that he stepped back. She said, "Mr. Parr, will you please tell Karen's father and these other gentlemen the conditions of Margo Llewelyn's will?"

Harry and I flashed each other a triumphant look. He snapped on the desk light and said, reading from something, "Louise Littleton is the appointed guardian, financial and in all other respects, of Margo Llewelyn's three daughters. The trust fund of each child will be administered by her in accordance with the will of the desceased as executed by me in February of this year."

The classic pin could have been heard to drop.

Then Brimmer said, "Bravo."

Billy said, "Well, gee, I guess that's that."

Shugrue said, "I'll fight it!"

"Yes, I thought you might, Mr. Shugrue." Harry opened his wallet. "Here's my card. I also have an office in Boston if that's more convenient."

"*I'll fight it beginning tomorrow!*"

"Oh, not tomorrow!" cried Louise involuntarily. "Tomorrow is commencement!"

I couldn't help smiling as the poor dear looked more distressed than she had through the whole awful business.

Shugrue was angrily out the door, slamming it. Then as Billy stood up, Brimmer unexpectedly sat down for the first time since he'd arrived. Louise and Harry and I exchanged puzzled looks as he leaned back, crossed his legs, and settled himself comfortably.

Billy, standing uncertainly beside his chair, said, "Well . . . I guess . . . I'll be going. . . ."

Louise walked to him. She said, "Mr. Venus, do you realize that you have a very bright little girl?"

He looked astonished. "No kidding?"

"Last March when Duff"—she caught herself—"when her mother brought her here, we put Christine in the first grade. She has done so well that the teachers have recommended her for a program we have called Bright Child Attention."

Billy gaped. "What do you know? My kid smart!"

Louise held out her hand to him. "Will you call me in a week or two? Christine will be back here, and I think we should ask her if she might want to visit you for a while. Would you like that?"

Billy got his hand connected with hers. "Sure. Sure I would. So . . . I'll call. . . ."

"Good-bye for now."

He looked around the room with the closest thing to a beam that bleariness would allow and said, "Can you beat that? My kid *smart*."

He left, and I thought nervously of those two men, one in a rage and the other in his cups, heading out through a dark downpour into unfamiliar surroundings. Would they get where they were going? Harry and Louise and I looked at Patrick Brimmer. What would *his* exit line be?

But he showed no sign of moving and only said, "Mrs. Littleton, I assume—and hope—you plan to keep my daughter here at school. To be quite frank, I wouldn't have the faintest idea what to do with her."

Callous-seeming words but not callously spoken, only gravely.

Louise said, after a second or two, "Are you married, Mr. Brimmer?"

"I was for a few years after Margo Llewelyn divorced me. I'm not now."

"Do you have other children?"

"No."

"Then yes, perhaps school would be best."

"But"—he stopped and sat forward, and I suddenly realized this man was under a strain; his cool was going. "You say commencement is tomorrow. Where would she—I mean, after that—what would I . . . ?"

Louise looked at him steadily. "We have a summer program." Did he hear the scorn in her voice? The can't-you-endure-your-child-for-one-summer?

But all he said was, "Thank you. Thank you very much," and stood up but stood still, UNFINISHED BUSINESS written all over him.

Harry kissed Louise with a flourish of finality. "Good night, my dear. The police will leave you alone till after graduation, then I'm afraid they'll descend again." He looked at Brimmer. "May I offer you a lift, Mr. Brimmer? Where are you staying?"

"Right down the road. The Woolcott Inn. And thank you, I have my car."

My turn to help ease him out. I stood up and said, "Louise, you're exhausted. I'm getting you to bed. Good night, Harry."

"Good night, Clara. Good night, Mr. Brimmer."

"Good night, Mr. Parr."

Every possible word of dismissal having been uttered, Harry shrugged and went to the door. He turned and smiled at Louise.

"I'll be so proud tomorrow."

"So will I." Louise's smile went from Harry to me, then graciously on to Brimmer. "Mr. Parr's granddaughter is the third generation to graduate from Woolcott Academy."

"Wonderful," I said.

"Indeed," said Brimmer.

Harry said pointedly, "Get a good night's rest, Louise."

He went out, and Brimmer said without moving, "But I'm afraid you won't."

Now, what the heck was this? The man was being a bore, overstaying his welcome and keeping us up. I said irritably, "You're afraid she won't what, Mr. Brimmer?"

"Get a good night's rest. Because of something I must tell her." He gazed at Louise as if she were some pitiful object, removed but involved. Then he looked at me. "Do I understand that you are Mrs. Littleton's lawyer?"

"No, I'm not. I'm here only as a friend."

"An old and trusted friend?"

"An absolutely trusted friend, Mr. Brimmer," said Louise, growing angry. "And I fail to see—"

"Because somebody other than you and I must know this. You can't bear it alone any more than I can. And I don't want the law or the police brought in because they wouldn't believe it now. But you two must. *You must believe it.*"

We stood nonplussed as this changed man walked about the room, and the rain drummed on the window, and the one light on the table between the chairs made him look like a shadowy intruder. Now he turned and faced us.

"Here it is: The dead woman in that hospital isn't Margo Llewelyn. It isn't Elaine Duffy. It's someone else."

8

"And if either of you," he went on violently and with scarcely a pause, "says to me, 'My dear man, you are irrational and raving,' I'll never forgive you. Do I appear to be raving? Yes, I probably do." He stood still, his hand to his head.

"Mr. Brimmer," I said, pushing Louise's stiffening form onto a chair, "What in God's name are you saying?"

"I know, I know . . . it's incomprehensible, and you're going to tell me—"

"I'm going to tell you," Louise interrupted abruptly, her face dead white, "to explain yourself."

"Yes. Yes, I will. Thank you."

His hand slid to the back of his neck, and he stood looking at the floor. I don't know what made me glance at my watch; perhaps a longing for this ghastly day to be over. Dear God, was it really only 10:30? I looked at Louise. She was motionless, staring fixedly at Brimmer, and he, finally, at her. I pulled a chair from somewhere and sat down at a tiny distance, conscious, despite my beclouded mind, of a subtle bond forming between them.

Brimmer said, sitting down, "I had almost made up my mind to walk out of here without saying anything. Then something happened. I heard you . . . call her Duff. I knew you'd been devoted friends. She used to speak of you. I also called her Duff."

He leaned forward, his hands clasped between his knees. His voice was calm now.

"Not only is the dead woman not Duff, I know exactly who she is. Her name is Violet La Grange, and for years she was Margo Llewelyn's stand-in. Violet was very proud of her job. She looked a lot like Duff, and she'd even had facial surgery to heighten the resemblance. She was somewhat older, so when Duff started to hit the skids, the likeness became quite uncanny. I saw Violet a year or so ago. She'd moved east and was living with her sister in Bridgeport, Connecticut. She came to see me. It was a very sad visit. I gave her some money."

Brimmer drew a breath and looked at me, then back at Louise. He went on carefully.

"There was a tiny physical difference between Duff and Violet that bears directly on what I'm saying. In fact, I rest my case on it." He was staring straight ahead. "It was Duff's birthday. We were in her dressing room. I'd bought her a pair of sapphire earrings and she went to the mirror to try them on and said, 'Oh, damn—not clip-on!' For some reason Duff always had a horror of having her ears pierced."

"I remember that," came from Louise's stiff lips.

"So now it was my turn to say, 'Oh, damn.' I'd forgotten. I said I'd have them altered, and just then Violet came in and in a moment of munificence I said, 'Give them to Vi, I'll get you a bracelet.' Vi looked thrilled, but Duff threw the earrings in her jewelry box and sulked and that was the end of it. I never thought of the episode again. Till today." Brimmer took a step back. "Violet was wearing those earrings when she was murdered this afternoon."

I moistened my lips. "How do you know? I can't believe they were left on her ears."

"They weren't. I asked the attendant at the hospital if I could see what had been on the body, and he brought everything out. I didn't need to see the earrings or the pierced ears. I knew the minute I looked at her it wasn't Duff."

We sat in silence. Then I said, more or less thinking out loud, "So, assuming your theory is valid, either Duff relented or Violet stole them. Not that it matters now."

"Not that it matters now," Brimmer repeated dully.

"But surely"—Louise was out of her chair—"there was identification on the body!"

"It was loaded with identification." Brimmer looked at her calmly. "But the woman is still Violet, not Duff."

His certainty was remarkable, but could it be trusted?

"I don't believe it." Louise closed her eyes. "If I were to—to look at her . . . would I know it isn't Duff?"

"I'm certain of it. In fact, I wish you'd—"

"No!" She shuddered violently. "No." Her eyes flew open. "Then other people will know it too! They're planning to hold one of those awful affairs where people are allowed to walk by and look—"

"Louise," I said, "Harry Parr said—"

"And if what you say is true," she went on wildly, "it will be horrible when somebody suddenly—"

"Mrs. Littleton," said Brimmer, and I stopped and listened because everything the man said fascinated me, "when the makeup people get through with that poor dead face, believe me, no one will know it isn't Margo Llewelyn."

I said, "May I get a word in edgewise?" They looked at me. "No public viewing, no visitation, no—in the words of our friend Mr. Shugrue—no *nothin'*. Cremation following the inquest."

Louise took this in with a gasp of relief. "Mr. Parr told you that?" I nodded. "Thank God!" She stood up, pushing the hair back from her face. "We must go to the police at once."

"I beg you not to." Brimmer was up again.

She stared at him. "*Why?* If this gruesome theory of yours is true—"

"You both say 'theory.' Fact. And it's the least important part of the question. The zinger is . . . where's Duff?"

I'd been waiting for this. I said, "Yes. Is she alive or dead? And who was meant for murder, Margo Llewelyn or Violet La Grange?"

Louise stood there helplessly, her hands at her side. I got up and walked to her desk. I shoved papers around looking for something. Louise was saying, "Everything was so right, so according to schedule. Her cable arrived this morning saying she'd pick up the girls and couldn't wait to see me."

"Here it is," I said and stood staring at Celestra's neat handwriting. "That's odd. . . ."

"What?" Brimmer was across the room and at my side in an instant.

"The signature."

He snatched it from me and read aloud, "Signed, Margo Llewelyn." He dropped it on the desk and looked at Louise. "Would Duff in one million years have signed herself to you 'Margo Llewelyn?' "

Louise stood mute. Brimmer leaned toward her across the desk. "When she wrote to you or to the children, how *did* she sign herself?"

"She never wrote once. Just sent presents."

"Where did the presents come from?"

"From England."

"She said she was going there?"

"Yes. She came to see me in the morning and was leaving that night."

"Easy enough to check. Do you remember the date she came to see you?"

Louise nodded.

Brimmer began to pace as Harry had paced a few hours before. Why must men pace? Then he said, "Of course, Violet could have gone on that plane in her place and come back in her place. Duff's passport was in her belongings."

I said, probably irritably, "Do sit down, Mr. Brimmer. I can't think with you striding about."

Louise, supportive though still dazed, said, "Mrs. Gamadge has been involved with crime before."

"Always as an amateur," I said quickly, as Brimmer looked at me in astonishment, "and never in a situation with such media hype. But if you wouldn't mind some input—"

"Of course!" And he did sit.

For a big shot, the man was very decent and sincere, though I still hadn't made up my mind if he was crazy or not. Of course, Margo's few, baffling, blurry contacts with the school since her departure certainly supported his bizarre theory.

"It seems to me," I said, "that the important question is this: if there was a switch, and I must repeat *if*—forgive my reservation, Mr. Brimmer—if there was one, when did it take place? When Duff left this school last March? When she returned here today? Or some time in between."

"Or," said Brimmer quietly, "—and forgive *my* reservation, Mrs. Gamadge—was the switch made *before* last March?"

We both looked at him in puzzlement.

Brimmer got up and went to Louise. He stood before her and said, "Are you sure the woman who came to see you that day *was* Duff?"

She looked at him almost serenely. "Yes. I'm as sure that woman was Duff as you're sure the dead woman isn't."

"Second the motion," I said.

Brimmer looked at me. "You saw her, too?"

"Yes."

He turned away and said revealingly, "That was a dumb question. As if anybody could mistake . . . the real Duff."

Louise burst out suddenly, "Oh, dear God, where is she? Is she—could somebody be holding her somewhere while this imposter came to take her children?" She sat down, her head in her hands.

"Or," said Brimmer, "is she in hiding someplace, and did she send Violet to impersonate her?"   .

"No." Louise looked up, and her voice was firm. "No. Duff would never do that to her children."

"I'm inclined to agree with you," he said. So was I.

"We *must* go to the police!" Louise was up again.

"Not yet, not yet." Brimmer's pacing began again. "Remember, a woman has been murdered, and the murderer must be found. That's all that concerns the police—for now." He stopped and stood looking at us. There was an element of unreality in the fact of his pleasant, familiar face, disturbingly transplanted from the television screen to this room and confronting us somberly. "Only we three have this . . . this other burden. Thank you for sharing it with me. I think I'd have gone mad alone with it." Now he was brisk again. "Mrs. Littleton, this person who discovered the body, was it someone here at the school?"

"My secretary."

"Would it be possible to speak to her?"

"Certainly not now!"

"Now. Right now."

"Absolutely not." Louise looked at him indignantly. "That poor woman is in shock, Mr. Brimmer. She's emotionally unstable as it is, and she's a borderline religious fanatic. She might—"

"She might be able to tell us something that would be meaningless to the police, but with our special knowledge—which we wouldn't reveal to her, of course—"

"It's out of the question." Louise turned her back on him.

Brimmer looked at me and put his hands together in a prayerful gesture. Actually, I was longing to talk to Celestra myself.

"Mr. Brimmer," Louise's voice was cold as ice, "I'm going to be very honest with you." She leaned against her desk and folded her arms. "When Harry Parr told me that you and . . . and . . . the others were coming here tonight, I decided to keep this fact firmly in mind: any one of you could have put that knife in Duff's back."

He looked at her thoughtfully. "Yes—except for Venus. If he was at that pool in California with other people, he's in the clear. But Shugrue and I haven't a leg to stand on. You would be perfectly justified in thinking I killed that woman believing her to be Duff."

"Having been so careless," Louise began to crack, "as not to have examined her ears first!"

It was the kind of half laughing, half crying state that overtakes one when frustration and exhaustion set in. I hurried to her and let her hang onto me.

Brimmer stood aghast, looking, for a moment, as if he might flee, then he moved a little toward us and said disjointed things like "I'm sorry—Oh, God, why did I have to—I should have kept my mouth shut—why didn't I just—" and finally a whole, revealing sentence: "But it's Duff! It's because it's Duff!"

And it dawned on me that he had probably never stopped loving her.

Louise wiped her eyes and simmered down.

I said, as innocently as I could, "You know, Louise, you did say you wanted to see Celestra. Why don't we go over there now? I'm sure Mr. Brimmer will be the soul of tact."

"The soul!" he breathed.

"And I'm certain Celestra wants to see you."

Louise looked at her watch. "But it's so late."

"Maybe that's good," I said, at least feeling honest about this. "You know how awful it can be at night if you're in a turmoil. And if she's asleep, we'll leave."

"At once," said Brimmer virtuously.

"Well"—Louise pushed away from the desk—"*I'm* not going to sleep tonight, that's one sure thing, so we may as well . . . Is it still raining?" She went to the window. "No, it's stopped."

Brimmer was all bustle. "If it's very far, my car is—"

"No, it's just a step. Clara—"

"Er—you two go ahead." My mind had suddenly veered in another direction. "I'll catch up with you. I'm going upstairs to the bathroom."

I wanted to be alone.

9

Alone to think.

I'd barely had time to since—since when? Since I had rushed to Louise—how many hours ago? And now this frightful development.

I sat down.

Was Patrick Brimmer insane? A liar? A . . . murderer? And if none of these, was he justified in asking that such a nightmare be kept to this room? Yes, murder had been done and the murderer was at large, and if Brimmer was wrong, it didn't much matter. It only mattered—and mattered horribly—if Margo Llewelyn was alive . . . or namelessly dead.

I stood up. Duff, you beautiful, bad, baffling troublemaker . . . where in God's name are you?

I sat down.

Was this fair to Harry? Surely he had the right to know. And yet . . . and yet . . . if it turned out to be an insane false alarm, better keep it only to the three of us.

I stood up.

It was the wrong move bringing Tina here tomorrow. How could Louise concentrate? And there was the crazy fact of commencement—I'd forgotten that.

I sat down.

Call Tina now. My watch said almost midnight, but young people never go to bed.

I stood up.

I punched numbers on the phone, and Tina said hello.

"Tina, don't come tomorrow. Go to the ball game. Come Monday. Can you get off?"

"I guess so. It's for business, after all. Why not tomorrow?"

"Louise has decided to go ahead with commencement so—"

"*Commencement?*"

"Yes, it's tomorrow. Didn't I mention that?"

"My God, it'll be one to remember."

"Louise feels she owes it to the graduates."

"That's guts."

"I think so. In addition"—careful here, Clara—"it doesn't look as if she'll need you this minute. All three of the children's fathers have been here, and only one is likely to—"

"*All three?*"

"Yes, they descended en masse."

"With their lawyers, I presume? What's Patrick Brimmer like—gorgeous?"

"Yes, rather. No lawyers. Actually, they—"

"Is Margo Llewelyn's lawyer there?"

"Yes."

"Man or woman?"

"Man." Oh, Lord, help me out of this.

"He'll handle the difficult papa. Is it Brimmer, or one of those slobs she married?"

"One of the slobs."

"What's his problem?"

"Tina, I can't talk."

"Okay. But if you're not going to do any investigating, I wish you'd get out of there. You're eating yourself up over those kids. Just scram."

"I plan to." I was holding on to my voice. "Tell Hen I hope his team wins. Good night."

"Clara, wait. Listen to me." I waited, and I listened. "Henry and I have been talking, and Sadd called from Florida an hour ago. We're unanimous. If you really don't intend to do anything on the case, you should leave. You don't owe Margo Llewelyn one more bloody damn thing."

Did you hear that, Duff? I said, "I know, dear. Good night."

I didn't exactly "bury my face in my hands," but I did put my fingers over my eyes for a minute and stand in the darkness trying to replace baleful images with benign ones such as my grandchildren wallowing in sand and sunshine on Cape Cod next week; but this only evoked visions of Duff's children wallowing in strife and uncertainty next week and every week. . . .

Sheer exhaustion, I told myself sternly, walking to the door. Now I was hoping Celestra *would* be asleep. I'd be back here and in bed in a flash. I walked out past the patrolman on duty and down the steps of the house.

The school grounds were well lighted, glistening wet, quiet but charged with tension. There were silhouettes, voices, and here and there a flashlight sparked as the police moved about. A light shone in the window of the little infirmary, which hadn't changed location since Paula's day. It was on the second floor of a small building that also housed several faculty members. Hadn't Jim said Celestra boarded here, too? Yes, the light over the door shone on a small car with the bumper sticker GOD LOVES YOU.

I went up three steps, and a glass window beside the door showed me a policeman. He opened the door.

"Mrs. Littleton said to go right up, ma'am."

A short flight, the waiting room, and beyond, a glimpse of beds and the little white-tiled dispensary. On a sofa beside Louise, Celestra sat hunched in a heavy parka. Her face was ravaged, her eyes enormous. Brimmer leaned in the shallow bay of the one window of the room.

"Look who's come to see you," said Louise brightly. "You remember Mrs. Gamadge."

"Oh, yes." The enormous eyes were trained on me. "You were here the day she brought the children, weren't you?"

"I guess I was at that. Imagine you remembering, Celestra." No question of who "she" was or what day or what children. Three of us were steeped in the recollection. Brimmer pushed a chair near the sofa, and I sat down with the feeling I hadn't missed much.

Louise said, "We've been talking about the days when Celestra was a student here, and I've been telling Mr. Brimmer how proud and grateful we are that she's given her whole life to Woolcott—"

"Mr. Brimmer is Louise's father, Mrs. Gamadge." Celestra interrupted suddenly. "He says he plans to leave her here at school. Isn't that wonderful?"

"It certainly is." I gave Louise's father the smile of the newly introduced.

"And maybe the two other girls will stay too. I've been praying for that." She clasped her hands in a beseeching gesture, and Louise put one of her own over them.

I looked with compassion at the drawn, rather pretty face. I have several very deeply religious friends. What separates them from the Celestras of this world? When does devoutness become obsession, blotting out every other consideration?

From the dispensary a middle-aged woman appeared, pulling a raincoat over her white uniform. She said, "Are you sure, Mrs. Littleton?"

"I'm positive. I'll sleep right in there next to her."

"There's medication on the counter. She should have some before she goes down."

"All right. And I know today is your last day, Mrs. Antoole. Have a nice summer."

"What about . . . ?" The woman nodded toward Celestra.

"We'll arrange something. Don't worry. Good night."

We echoed this, and she left. Now I got it: we need to be alone to conduct our unofficial inquiry. Brimmer pulled up another chair and sat down.

Celestra began to cry. "Mrs. Littleton, you shouldn't have to sleep here. I'm fine. I'm really—"

"But I want to." Louise smiled and did some hand patting. "I haven't spent a night in the infirmary since I was at school here. It will be fun, and we can talk." The patting continued. "Would you mind talking a little right now?"

"No." Celestra dropped her head back against the sofa. There was a limpness about her now. With the nurse gone, the room occupied only by friends, and above all, her idol beside her, she must have been feeling something like peace for the first time since the heavens fell in upon her.

Louise and Brimmer both looked at me with a "you're on" expression. Me and all my big fat experience. I was rather at a loss . . .

"Celestra," I began, "we know the police have been asking you a lot of questions, and you must be—"

"But I didn't answer them. It was too awful to talk about, and they said I didn't have to right now."

"You don't, that's true." I cast about. "In fact, that's why we came to see you. We thought it might be easier for you to talk to us first."

"Oh, yes. I *want* to talk to you." Her head dropped on the shoulder beside her.

Louise said, "If any of our questions upset you, we'll stop."

"Okay." Eyes closed.

I swallowed, not sure that the first words out of my mouth wouldn't be upsetting in the extreme; but there was no way to duck them.

"When you first saw Margo Llewelyn's body, what did—"

"Well, you wouldn't exactly call it her *body*"—Celestra's eyes opened and fixed on the ceiling—"because that usually means a *dead* body, and when I first saw her she was getting out of the taxi."

Getting out of the . . . ? I sat forward. Louise and Brimmer were perfectly still.

"You saw her alive?" I said.

"Oh, yes."

I looked at my cohorts, and they looked at me. For the moment, I literally couldn't speak.

Brimmer said, hoarsely I thought, "Where was the taxi?"

"It was just turning into the school grounds." Celestra's head came up with a jerk, and her voice turned harsh. "I knew she was here to take the children, and that was the end of any religion for the poor little . . ."

Oh, God! Oh, God! Oh, God!

Celestra was still talking, and they were still listening, but was it with the same horror as I? My mouth went perfectly dry. I got up and moved toward the dispensary and water.

"And I heard her tell the driver to go ahead up to the school and get the children, and she'd wait there on the bench—you know, the one by the gate. She said to hurry."

Silence. When Louise spoke, her voice told me she knew. "What . . . happened . . . then?"

I was at the sink, running water hard, hoping I wouldn't hear, but I did.

"I started talking to her. I thought it was terrible she wasn't going to see you and say good-bye, and I told her so. I said she should leave the girls here so they could get a good education with some religion in it, and she just laughed. When I said I really meant it, she told me to mind my own business. That's when I went over to the kitchen and got the knife. I didn't let anybody see me take it; they wouldn't understand. But I knew God would. I knew he didn't want the girls to go back to that awful Hollywood."

I couldn't bring myself to turn around. I stood drinking water, staring at a roll of paper toweling.

"She didn't even hear me come up behind her. . . . Then I pulled her over to the bushes because I heard the taxi coming back. The driver said where was she because the school wouldn't let the children go with just him, and I said she'd gone, and he was mad because he hadn't been paid." The weary head went back against the sofa again. "After he left, I began to feel awful, even though I knew I'd pleased God by doing what I did. But it was so hard and terrible. . . . And that's when I ran to you."

I went back into the room with a glass of water. Brimmer had stood up, and now he moved to the chair I'd occupied and more or less fell into it. Louise was rigid except for a mechanical, jerky stroking of the clasped hands beside her. Our dazed tableau held for a few seconds, then I went to Louise and put her other hand around the glass. Her lips formed "Thanks" and she drank some water. We looked at the exhausted face, eyes closed, mouth slightly agape.

Brimmer said quietly, "Purged and at peace." He got up and came and stood beside me. "Classic dementia. You serve God by slaying the infidels."

Louise whispered, looking up at us pitifully, "Police?"

"Harry Parr first," I said. "He'll have to handle it."

"But not tonight, please not tonight." She was half weeping. "We'll call him in the morning. I want to get her to bed."

Brimmer and I exchanged a look. He moved back as Louise stood up and patted the wan cheek. She said, "You deserve a good night's sleep." Celestra opened her eyes and smiled and nodded and let us take her into the next room.

There were half a dozen beds. I remembered Paula being in one of them with the flu. Would anyone have thought these quiet, healing quarters would ever harbor a mad, sad murderer? I went into the dispensary for the medication, and Brimmer came to the door.

"It's out of the question for Mrs. Littleton to stay here alone," he said.

"It's out of the question for her to stay here at all."

"But she will." He leaned on the door. "I'm willing to bet she won't leave that poor creature."

"That poor creature is also a homicidal maniac. Strictly speaking, what we should do is call Harry Parr right this minute."

"Yes, we should, but . . ."

"But we won't because Louise begged us not to and she's in great torment."

"So the next best thing"—he straightened—"is for me to sit in a chair in the doorway of that room and never close my eyes. It's only a few more hours till morning. Then we *must* call Parr."

I hesitated, but had to say it. "Will you keep mum till he makes the report?"

"Of course."

"For a guy who's business is news you're being slightly magnificent."

He shrugged. "Where are you staying?"

"At the Head's house."

"Go back and go to bed. Give me that stuff." He held out his hand, and I put the bottle into it. "Good night."

He went through one door, and I went out the other.

As I recrossed the school grounds, the clouds dispersed and the moon shone. I noticed an odd, skeletal structure on the hockey field. I asked the policeman who stopped me and wanted my name, what it was.

"Portable bleachers, ma'am. They're holding commencement here tomorrow."

"Commencement." The word was assuming the cloak of black comedy in the midst of tragedy.

10

I never—well, in the words of the captain of the *Pinafore*, "hardly ever"—take sleeping medicine. I think I'm afraid that if I sleep too late I'll miss something. But in this case I'd have gladly missed the entire next day. Unhappily, the single pill that I carry with me in case of dire need took me only till half past ten the next morning. I came to, dazed and longing for coffee.

As I lay in bed, spooked by yesterday's events, and wondering whether to struggle over to the dining hall, I heard feet, several pairs, mounting the stairs. They went past my room and down the hall. A woman spoke, gently, reassuringly, and a man—Harry?—urgently. The door of Louise's room opened and closed, and steps came back. A knock—a thump actually—and Harry put his head in.

"You'd better be decent, Clara. My God, isn't this ghastly?"

He held a cup of coffee in an unsteady hand. I grabbed my robe and the precious brew. "Harry, how can I thank you!"

"Thank Louise. She said to bring it. Mrs. Owens and I just brought her over, and she's been put to bed till the ceremonies at two o'clock. Needless to say, she didn't sleep a wink in that infirmary." His face was very white. "I can barely take it in, Clara."

"I know. I know. Sit down." He did, dazedly. I sipped the lukewarm coffee gratefully. "When did Louise call you?"

"She didn't. Patrick Brimmer did. He phoned me at seven o'clock. I wasn't even awake. I'm not sure I am now. It's a nightmare."

"What did Brimmer say?" I sat on the side of the bed.

"He said to come to the school infirmary at once, that Louise was there and needed me." Poor Harry shook his head. "I couldn't imagine what he was doing there. Didn't he leave last night?"

"Not really." I hastened on. "How does Celestra seem this morning? Did you speak to her?"

"Yes, at length. We went into the kitchen and Brimmer made coffee and then left. Louise told Celestra she must say nothing of her action to *anyone*—needless to say, Louise's word is law to her—and that we thought it best for her to go to the hospital for a few days' rest. I called my friend Dr. Metcalf at the psychiatric wing and he agreed to take her for 'observation.' I simply said the woman was suffering from stress. We have to keep this awful thing to ourselves until tonight."

"Tonight?"

"Then I'll go to the police."

I was puzzled and uneasy. "Why the wait, Harry? The woman has killed somebody."

His face became set and stubborn. "She's killed somebody whom she believed to be a deadly enemy of God. She's not likely to meet another such person between now and eight o'clock tonight. I'll go to the police directly from the graduation dinner. That's the windup. Woolcott Academy is going to be closed and empty before it gets another broadside from the media."

Despite my unease, I was touched by this display of loyalty

and affection for Wooly. Not many schools today engender this kind of devotion, I thought, as we sat in silence. Harry leaned back in his chair, then leaned forward. He seemed to find no comfortable position. Finally, he hung over the side of it and looked at me earnestly.

"The whole thing is so damn weird that I'm worried the police won't believe it. They may think Celestra is a kook confessing to a crime she didn't commit."

"I thought of that." I stood up wishing I'd brought a warmer robe. I was suddenly cold. "Fortunately—or unfortunately—her prints must be all over that knife."

Harry sat staring at the carpet. I was longing to ask him the question that Patrick Brimmer had put to Louise and me. But would it only deepen his distress? Perhaps some chitchat first. . . . I got up and went to the window.

"I hope commencement goes off well. Louise deserves it."

"It should." He got up and joined me. The sound of hammering reached us. In the bright sunshine the bleachers were being erected. "The police are being very cooperative. They're setting up a detour for a few hours. Only guests' cars can come to the school entrance, and people have to identify themselves."

A bit more small talk about the ceremony, then, "Harry, you've been wonderful. You must be exhausted. And you do have other clients."

He shook his head. "I'm semiretired. But I have to get to the airport. My wife's been visiting in New York, and she's coming back for Gable's graduation."

"Gable?"

"My granddaughter. She has her mother's maiden name."

"It's charming." Now for my question. "By the way, tell me something: when Duff came to your office last February, did she . . . seem like her old self?"

"Her old self?"

"I mean—and of course she was forty-five and not sixteen—but—and I'm just curious—would you have known right away that it was Duff?"

"Oh, yes. And for a funny reason." Harry smiled and looked across the room. "Remember I told you the first time she ever saw me she kissed me? Well, when my secretary said she was there, I found myself wondering—probably hoping—that she'd do it again."

"And she did."

He nodded and grinned. "No fool like an old fool. Oh"—he snapped his fingers and reached into his pocket—"that reminds me. I brought these with me this morning intending to give them to Brimmer and forgot."

A pair of sapphire blue earrings lay in his palm. I stared at them as he went on.

"When Duff was in my office that day, she used the phone. She kept changing the receiver from ear to ear, and finally she pulled these off and said something like 'Damn things, I never could wear them,' and then she said—and this would please Brimmer—'I only keep these because Patrick gave them to me.' Of course she forgot them, and I put them in the drawer to give her when she got back."

Harry took my hand and dropped the earrings into it. "Give them to Louise, will you? She can keep 'em or give 'em to Brimmer or whatever. Gosh, your hands are cold, Clara. I hope you're okay."

No, I was not okay. I was not remotely okay. I was hearing Brimmer's voice. *Those earrings were on the dead woman when she was found.* And in Harry's office at the same time? Fortunately, Harry was at the door saying he'd see me later. Then he was gone.

Shaking, I pulled on my clothes. Wait till I got my hands on

that Patrick Brimmer! Where was he? Gone back to the Woolcott Inn? Gone back to Connecticut? Gone back to his *nuthouse?*
Was he crazy after all? Or a killer?

I opened the door and started down the stairs. Louise's voice
stopped me. She was standing in her doorway clutching her robe
around her.

"Clara, it was so sad. She went off to the hospital like an
angel."

"Then not sad really. Go back to bed."

"I just thought of something."

"What, dear?" I remained on the steps, not wanting to
encourage any in-depth confidences with Brimmer's perfidy
and/or lunacy weighing on me.

"Bishop Staples. He's very elderly, and he has a bathroom
problem. He has to be escorted there and back, or he loses his
way. Will you tell Mr. Herman to keep the usual eye out?"

Who the heck was Mr. Herman, and my problem was bigger than the bishop's, but I said, "Will do" and hurried on. If
Brimmer didn't answer at the inn, I'd call his home, and either
he or his answering machine would get a blistering blast. Wherever he was . . .

He was standing at Louise's desk talking on the phone and jot-
ting something on a pad. He hung up and said, "Good morning.
I'm doing a bit of research."

"So am I." I walked up to him and opened my hand. "Are
these the earrings you mentioned?"

He looked down at them, then up at me. "Yes."

"Will you please explain how they could have been on the
dead woman yesterday and in Harry Parr's desk drawer since last
February?"

He was blank. "I can't. Where did you get them?"

I laid the earrings on the desk and launched into a scathing repeat of Harry's account. When I got to "pulled these off," Brimmer turned and seized them.

"They've been changed! They're not for pierced ears anymore."

It was my turn to seize. I hadn't examined them. Sure enough, they were clip-ons.

We stood staring at each other. I said, "Two pairs?" as the door opened and Jim put a foot in.

"There's somebody here from the hospital."

The hospital! Celestra had gone berserk! No such thing. An attractive, smiling woman in a white uniform came in holding out her hand to me. She said, "You must be Mrs. Littleton. There's a very worried person out here who is sure—"

"It's the diplomas!" Celestra pushed past her. "I never finished them!"

She hurried to a file cabinet and pulled it open. The nurse was still smiling patiently. "I hope we haven't disturbed you, Mrs. Littleton, but the doctor thought it best to let Celestra reassure herself so we drove over."

"Of course." I had taken her hand rather bewilderedly. "My name is Clara Gamadge. Mrs. Littleton is resting. This is Patrick Brimmer."

"Yes, I recognized you." She smiled appreciatively. "I'm Alma Lang."

Brimmer extended his hand to the nurse but looked at me in astonishment, probably wondering, I realized, why Celestra was essentially still at large.

I explained to him hastily, "Harry Parr thought Celestra needed a few days' rest before that—er—important business has to be done."

He nodded, enlightened, I hoped, as Celestra turned triumphantly waving a folder.

"I knew it! Three more names to do! I'll just sit right down at my desk. And then they have to be rolled and tied—thank goodness I remembered the ribbon! Maybe some of you would help with that?"

Her eager glance circled us and landed on the desk. "Oh, there are her pretty blue earrings!"

Brimmer was at the nurse's side like lightning. He drew her across the room, and I heard his solicitous questions about her patient. I positioned myself between them and Celestra and said in a low voice, "You've seen these before, Celestra?"

"Yes, I noticed them especially because I love blue stones, and I asked her if they were real sapphires, and she said . . . she said . . . oh, dear, I can't repeat what she said because it was a swear word—I'll spell it: she said 'No, d-a-m-n it, they're fake and just my luck.' "

In my elation, I nearly let Celestra babble on, but the nurse's presence was too risky. So far I was pretty sure she'd heard nothing. I said, "Mrs. Littleton will be so grateful you remembered the diplomas, Celestra. You'd better get working on them," and she hurried to the door. The nurse gave me a sad, "poor thing" shrug, and they went out.

Brimmer was back at my side. "That's it. Two pairs. One pair's a fake."

"That's it! *D-a-m-n it*, that's it!" I think I gave a little skip. "We don't say a swear word—we *spell* it. But Violet didn't spell it when she told Celestra the pretty blue stones were fake. I guess she'd had them appraised." I picked up the earrings and put them in his hand. "It seems obvious. Duff had a cheap pair made for Violet—you'd said she could have them—and altered the originals because—"

"Because they were worth a thousand dollars." Brimmer turned away.

"I doubt that a thousand dollars meant much to Duff in her glory days. She told Harry she kept them because you gave them to her."

The effect of these words was a change in his expression to one of utter sadness. I moved away and sat down—gratefully. I felt as if I'd been thrust, protesting, onto a roller coaster and had survived the first dive, but still had to endure the rest of the ride. When I looked back at him, Brimmer was holding the earrings in his palm and gazing down at them.

I surprised myself by saying, "You've never stopped loving her."

"Never." It was said instantly and simply. He dropped the jewels into his pocket and moved to a chair but then just stood looking at it. "Even after she left me and her men got more and more disreputable and her habits more and more destructive, I wasn't so much angry as . . . disappointed."

Now he did sit down and looked at me almost musingly. The woman he spoke of seemed to materialize in the room.

"I always thought Duff had what I'd call *quality*. It was partly what made her a star, but mostly what made her a person. Of course, she was obsessed with her origins, which she considered disgraceful, and no amount of reassurance, or counseling, or . . . love could make her believe she was anything but a mongrel."

We sat in silence, then Brimmer sprang up. "*Was!* Why do I keep saying *was?* She may be alive and in need, and we're doing nothing about it!"

Well, thank you very much, I thought. I've only devoted the last twenty-four hours and my peace of mind to this mess.

Brimmer was at the desk. He picked up the paper he'd been writing on when I came in, and began hitting numbers on the phone. He said, "I got information in Bridgeport, Connecticut. Two 'La Granges' are listed. Let's hope one of them is related to Violet."

I suddenly had an overpowering desire to go back to bed. I leaned back in my chair and closed my eyes, and this is what I heard before I opened them again.

"Yes . . . hello . . . I wonder if you can help me. I'm trying to contact a woman named Violet La Grange. By any chance would you—I beg your pardon? This is Violet speaking?"

11

Brimmer pressed the cradle of the phone but continued to stand with the receiver in his hand. He looked at me and said, "Don't move."

"Don't worry. I can't."

He frowned into space, then released the cradle and hit numbers again, saying, "There's only one explanation." Then he spoke into the phone. "This is the person who just called asking for Violet La Grange. I don't know who you are, but you can't possibly be Violet because I just saw her an hour ago in Massachusetts." He stood still, listening. "Calm down, please. No, this is not the police. This is a friend. If you want to help her . . . yes, please do."

Again he stood listening. Sounds from the phone indicated a degree of hysteria. Finally Brimmer said, "I have no idea. I saw her quite by accident and very briefly. Sorry I can't help you." He hung up quickly and faced me.

"Her sister, fronting for her. It seems that three months ago Violet instructed her—in fact, paid her—to answer the phone and say she was Violet. The woman hasn't seen Violet since."

Three months ago. But which of them had gone to England, Margo Llewelyn or Violet La Grange? At the moment it was simply too much for me. If I was not to be allowed to sleep, at least I should be allowed to eat. I said, "I haven't had a bite of food since last night."

"My God, it's almost noon! Let me take you—"

"And yet"—now I was torn as well as hungry—"and yet . . . suppose Louise should suddenly need me. It makes me reluctant to leave." I walked to the window and looked out at the bustle of activity. "I know this sounds melodramatic, but I have the feeling that I'm standing between her and madness."

"You aren't! You are!" Brimmer laughed slightly and came toward me. "*Aren't* being melodramatic, *are* saving her from madness. Saving me too, Mrs. Gamadge, believe me."

For an instant, I allowed myself to bask, like Harry, in a no-fool-like-an-old-fool glow. This attractive, celebrated man had his hands on my shoulders and was telling me I was saving him from madness. I pulled up with a sigh and said, "Then will you get me something to eat?"

"I certainly will. In fact"—he started for the door—"I'll go to the inn. It's minutes away, and they have great food. I'll be back with the feast you deserve."

"Mr. Brimmer," I said, and he turned. "You must have a ton of commitments. You should go home."

He looked at me thoughtfully. "You know, I've been telling myself the same thing." And he left.

Scratchy sounds of band practice drew me to the window again. The dais was finished and decorated, rows of folding chairs in place, and the grounds bright with girls. "Students are requested to wear dresses for the commencement ceremonies" had been the directive in Paula's day; in mine it had been "At commencement ceremonies uniforms will be worn." (Not requested.) And next year there would be boys. The old order changeth—and I'd better changeth too, I thought, looking down at the skirt I'd dragged on this morning. First I'd check on who was holding the fort. I opened the door and beheld the consoling presence of officer Jim. He was chatting with Celestra and the nurse as they rolled the last diplomas. I started to say that I'd be upstairs for a few minutes, when I saw an appalling figure coming up the steps to the front door.

Frank Shugrue.

I almost panicked. Let his identity be revealed in Celestra's presence, and God knows what it might trigger! Hysterical pleas to leave his daughter here in school, leading to—Jim was stepping forward to request the name. I said, "I know this gentleman, Jim," and beckoned Shugrue into the office.

I turned as I closed the door and glared at him. "I think you're despicable, Mr. Shugrue, coming here today to hound—"

"Look—I got good news." His shoulders hunched inside his expensive, ugly clothes, and his rheumy eyes gazed around. "Where is she?"

"If you mean Mrs. Littleton, not only is she not available, she wouldn't dream of seeing you without her lawyer."

"We don't need no lawyer for this. Here's the good news: I ain't gonna bring no lawsuit."

His expression, insofar as I could decipher it in his destroyed face, was one of virtue triumphant.

I said, mustering sarcasm, "Oh, that is good news. Especially as it's unlikely you'd win."

"Don't be too sure!" He waggled a finger at me. "I could make life miserable for you people."

"Oh, you don't need a lawsuit for that, Mr. Shugrue. You're

doing fine right now." I started for the other door. "I'll tell Mrs. Littleton your good news. Now, if you'll excuse me—"

"A simple proposition, that's what I got." The word "proposition" stopped me. "I don't bring no suit, no bad publicity to the school, she keeps the kid, and settles a little something on me."

Dear God—blackmail? Had he discovered what Brimmer had? Don't be a fool, Clara. It's only a greedy gamble. But I had to know for certain. "Tell me if I'm right," I said. "Your proposition is that you'll sell your daughter to Mrs. Littleton for the right price."

He tried to look indignant. "That's not a real nice way to put it."

"No, but then it's not a real nice proposition." Challenging words, and if he had an ace, now was the moment to play it. But he didn't. All he had was a coarse and desperate apologia.

"Look: suppose I sue and suppose I even win, but then suppose I can't break the trust, so what have I got? Lawyers' fees and an eight-, nine-year-old kid on my hands."

"I thought Karen was ten" were the only words to come through my tight lips.

"See! You people know more about her than I do." Shugrue ran a finger around his collar. "For a little financial consideration I'd even put her back in this school." He looked around moodily. "There must be a lot of kids here their parents don't know what the hell else to do with them."

I'd stopped wincing at his words, and the last were so true that I had to give him another minute.

"Yes, every boarding school has some of those. Mrs. Littleton was one herself."

He looked astonished. "No kidding? Her parents too?"

"Oh, they were dead. It was her grandparents who didn't know what the hell else to do with her." I looked at the man's deathly sick face. "I'll put your sordid proposition to Mrs. Littleton. Good-bye."

I started toward the stairs. Shugrue said to my departing back, "Oh, by the way, when I left here last night I decided to do what Brimmer did. I figured if he could take it I could. I went to that hospital and looked at her."

I froze. Had he deliberately saved his ace?

He added, as he went to the door and through it, "Boy, did she look *old!*"

Relief and disgust flooded me—also a need for air. After a second or two I followed him, went past the trio in the outer office, and from the steps watched Shugrue get into a waiting cab. It drove away past cars already arriving, tooting, girls running to them. I looked at my watch: 1:00. I was starving. Where was my promised feast?

The door behind me opened, and Celestra came out carrying a basket of diplomas. She said proudly, "All ready for the bishop."

The bishop! He of the problem! I said, "Celestra, where does the bishop go when he arrives?"

"Oh, he and Mrs. Staples always come here first and visit with Mrs. Littleton—besides he usually needs the bathroom. I should remind Mr. Herman about that." She frowned. "I wonder where he . . ."

"We'll find him." The nurse took her arm. "And you said you wanted to change."

"Oh, yes. I can't sit on the dais in this old thing. You see, it's my job to hand the diplomas to the bishop as the girls come up. See you later, Mrs. Gamadge."

I smiled at her, and Celestra, followed by her shadow, trotted down the steps. The devoted acolyte hurrying to perform a sacred rite. . . . Ah, Brimmer and food!

His car buzzed up to the steps, and I waved and went inside. I said to Jim, "Will you help Mr. Brimmer bring in some stuff?"

"Sure." He started out.

"Er . . . Jim . . . have you any idea how the investigation is going?"

"I understand tomorrow they're starting to bring in people from the school for questioning."

No need, no need, I thought somberly. By tomorrow the blow would have fallen, but at least, thanks to Harry, it would fall on empty, echoing halls.

I went into the office, looked around, and found a card table behind a bookcase. Brimmer and Jim came in fragrantly ladened, and Jim retired with a share.

Brimmer said, "You must be famished. I certainly am. Do you suppose Mrs. Littleton has eaten? Where is she, by the way?"

"Right here," said her voice, "and no I haven't eaten, and I smell something heavenly."

She was coming down the stairs and now appeared in a beautiful white dress, her cap and gown over her arm. She threw them across a chair and added, "So I hope I'm invited."

"You are," said Brimmer, "if you can supply a corkscrew."

"In that drawer."

It was almost fun, certainly it was conspiratorial and congenial. Louise looked lovely, Brimmer looked impressed, and I looked from one to the other. Hmmmmm . . .

We pulled chairs to the table and unloaded cartons. Brimmer said the chef at the inn had suggested a Chablis to go with his special chicken and dumplings; the marrons glacés and the Amaretto coffee were his own idea.

Louise said suddenly and sadly, "If Celestra was here, she'd say grace."

"Then let's," I said.

A nice thought, but who would implement it? Brimmer said,

"I give you one from Camp Arrowhead, Maine, circa 1965: Bow wow wow, thanks for the chow."

Our laugh dispelled the shadow, and we fell to. By what seemed to be silent agreement, we didn't talk about Duff. Louise said she'd called St. Cecelia House just before she came downstairs and talked to both Sister Beranice and the Manettis. The girls were fine but wanted to come back to Wooly, a good sign, she hoped. Brimmer said he wondered if his daughter would recognize him next time she saw him, and I gave them an account of Frank Shugrue and his "proposition."

Brimmer said, "What nerve. He's almost as bad as I am, except that I don't want my child's money. And if I did, I couldn't get it." He buttered a roll. "Shugrue hasn't a chance in hell of breaking that trust, and he knows it. Besides, suppose Duff . . ."

He stopped buttering, and we all stopped eating. Suppose Duff . . . reappeared.

Louise picked up her wineglass and sat back in her chair. She said, "This is preposterous. Will you kindly consider my situation, since Duff apparently never bothered to?" She frowned angrily and sipped. "I was married twenty-five years ago for a few weeks. I never had any children. I now find myself saddled—if you'll excuse the expression"—Brimmer reached for his glass—"with three children, two of whom appear to be permanent fixtures. When—"

A knock, and Jim looked in. "Will you see Mr. Venus, ma'am?"

Not possible. We looked at each other, and Brimmer said, "*Three* permanent fixtures?" and buried his face in his napkin. Choking? Laughing? Crying?

From the foyer, Billy's quite sober-sounding voice called plaintively, "I won't stay five minutes, Mrs. Littleton."

She nodded to Jim, and he stepped back. Billy passed him almost at a skip. He looked surprisingly spruce.

95

Louise picked up her fork again and said, "Mr. Venus, I seem to recall telling you that you could come for Christine in two weeks."

"But see—that's the point—I don't want to—I mean, I *can't* come for her."

More sounds from behind Brimmer's napkin. Billy stammered on. "See . . . something happened, and I changed my mind. That is—"

"Let me help you. Mr. Venus." I took a bite of salad. "You've decided that this is a really fine school, a really *very* fine school, and that on the whole it would be better to leave Christine in Mrs. Littleton's care because after all"—Shugrue's words rang in my ears—"what would you do with a seven-year-old girl?"

He fidgeted. "Yeah, well, sort of, but—"

"But"—Brimmer lowered his napkin and looked at the third husband of the woman he'd loved—"you wouldn't object to a few dollars of the money her mother—"

"I don't want Christine's money."

It was said quietly, and we were silent. Then Louise said, "What *do* you want, Mr. Venus?"

"Well, see"—Billy took an eager step toward her—"after I left here last night, I did what you did, Mr. Brimmer. I went to that hospital, and they let me look at her."

I sensed my tablemates holding their breath as I was.

"Gee . . . I remember when she was so beautiful."

Breathing was resumed, and Billy went on. "Well, there were these reporters there, and they remembered me from when I was, you know, big. And one of them said he had a friend in the business, and he thought maybe with Margo kind of big again—you know, because she's dead—well, he'd tell his friend he'd seen me and—guess what? This morning I got a call from Detroit and an offer for six weeks at a club there! Jeez, I mean, I can really thank Margo for that, can't I?"

Ghastly as it all sounded, Billy was oddly touching in his joy and gratitude. He went on rapidly, backing toward the door, "So if I'm working again, it wouldn't be possible to—"

The door opened behind him, and Jim announced, "Ma'am, there's an elderly Reverend out here looking for a bathroom."

"The bishop!" Louise jumped up. "And don't you dare go, Mr. Venus. I have a few things to say to you!" She headed out the door, and I headed up the stairs. Was it two o'clock already? I yanked a dress from the closet, gave my hair a swipe—trying, fascinated, to imagine the conversation between Patrick Brimmer and Billy Venus—and descended to learn that there hadn't been one. Billy had ducked out while Louise was showing the bishop to the facilities, and she now stood, flushed and angry before a mirror in the bookcase, adjusting her mortarboard. Brimmer was throwing trash into a plastic bag. She glared at him.

"Why didn't you stop that man?"

"Stop him?" Brimmer looked surprised. "Why? To lecture him on his parental delinquency? I'd be the pot calling the kettle black."

"You certainly would!"

She was shaking. I walked past them to the other door and went out, closing it behind me. A number of berobed faculty members and guests were assembling. I spotted Harry Parr and beckoned to him.

"Harry," I whispered, "she's very upset. Billy Venus was just here."

"I thought I recognized that character! What did he—"

"The bishop is in the bathroom."

"Where else?

"Who are these people?"

"Her faculty escort."

"Do this: tell them she's delayed, and herd them all over there. She has to have ten minutes."

97

Harry nodded. "I'll tell the band to play a bit longer, and then I'll come back for her."

"Bless you."

I went back inside. Louise was pulling on her robe with trembling hands, and Brimmer was pouring coffee into styrofoam cups. He said, "How do you ladies take it?"

"Cream, please," I said. "No sugar."

"I haven't got time," said Louise.

"Yes, you do." I took her arm and moved her gently to a chair. "Harry has everything under control including the bishop. He's explaining to your faculty escort that owing to—what's the expression?—the 'cruel and unusual punishment' you've endured, you'll be briefly delayed. He'll come back for you after everybody has heard 'Pomp and Circumstance' three times and liked it. Now, how do you take your coffee?"

"Black." She sat down almost meekly, and Brimmer handed her a cup. "Thank you. Sorry I blew up. I guess Mr. Venus appeared just a little too soon after Mr. Shugrue. And of course, we know your plans for *your* daughter, Mr. Brimmer." She took off her mortarboard and fanned herself with it.

"Oh, yes. Same as the others. To stick you with her."

I giggled weakly—perhaps I was getting punchy—and Louise even smiled a little.

Brimmer went on, "But I do hope to see the poor child more often than in the past. I'll have to brush up on fatherhood, though. I'm pretty rusty."

"At least you have something to brush up on! How would you like to be in my position? Sudden, surrogate motherhood—a triple dose—and no experience whatever!"

"But," I said, afraid I knew what her answer would be, "you've been surrounded by children all your professional life."

"Exactly. 'Surrounded,' not involved or directly responsible."

She replaced her headgear with an agitated slap. "I don't feel fit for it, I don't want it, and I'm scared. I'm *quaking*."

"So am I," said Brimmer quietly. "Maybe we'd better stay in touch and quake together."

The silence was short but charged. I looked into my coffee and let them look at each other.

Then Louise said, her voice trembling, "And where's the cause of it all? Oh, God, Duff, *where are you?*"

Harry appeared and said from the door, "Ready, my dear?"

12

Brimmer and I stood in the quiet room, and for the first time I heard the sound of the band which must have been playing for a while. Why had I bothered to change my clothes? I could no more walk over there and sit in that gala, gossiping crowd than . . .

"Is there any coffee left?" I asked.

"Sure is."

He poured two cups and handed me one. I took mine to the window and watched the distant figure of Louise mount the platform and smile around. Knowing the question that ate at her mind, I voiced it involuntarily: "Where? *Where is Duff?*"

There was silence behind me, then Brimmer said matter-of-factly, "Oh, Duff's dead."

My head jerked in his direction. "How do you . . . ?"

"Know? I don't, for certain." He swallowed his coffee and pitched the cup into the trash. "I just mean that I believe she's gone, and I'll tell you why and how."

He started to fold the card table, and I stood at the window looking alternately at him and at the blur of Louise on the dais. I had the sensation of being the link between two persons who had cared deeply for the same woman in years past and were now sharing grief and frustration at her . . . her what? "Evaporation" was an idiotic word, but yes, dammit, for lack of a better one, Duff had simply evaporated.

Brimmer sat down, stretched his legs, and looked at the ceiling. He said, "I've thought of nothing else—I'm sure you haven't either—since yesterday. It seems to me that what happened is this: Violet followed Duff to England, killed her, stripped the body of identification, and disposed of it. Don't ask me how, but it can and is often done. Then she simply took Margo Llewelyn's place." He sat forward studying the rug. "Claiming the children would be the perfect proof of identity."

I said, trying to follow his thinking, "You mean . . . when she picked them up, she planned to tell the girls their mother had sent her for them."

He nodded. "Then she'd have shipped them off to their fathers and gone into seclusion on Margo Llewelyn's money. Everybody knew the great has-been was prime for the role of recluse."

"But it's insane." I moved from the window. "How long did she think she could get away with the impersonation?"

"You don't ask yourself that when you've been living high on the hog for three months and now you must go back to Bridgeport and obscurity."

"Why" —I moved to the desk and stared down at the cable— "did Duff tell her where the children were? She didn't tell anyone else."

"I suppose she had to confide in somebody. I can hear her: 'Vi, if I freak out, this is where the kids are' and so forth."

I picked up the cable. "And only the intervention of a poor crazy woman spoiled the plan."

"Only that."

Back I went to the window. The bishop's address came squeaking faintly over the loudspeaker. Might it all come over Louise as she sat there? And when Celestra came forward with her basket of diplomas, might every aspect of our awful secret suddenly overwhelm her?

Brimmer stood up and looked about irresolutely.

"How do we end this?" I asked. "How do we rid Louise of it?"

He considered. "Rid her of it? Never, I'm afraid—or rid ourselves. But with Duff and Violet both dead, that's an end."

I felt sudden anger.

"I wish you had never come here! I wish you had stayed away and never said anything to anybody!"

"So do I. I should have simply lived with the damn thing myself."

It was said with such genuine remorse that I felt a pang. Why does anything in the nature of an apology always have an ameliorating effect?

"On the other hand," I said, "Louise is at least semi-prepared in the event that . . ." I started collecting cups. "You see, I don't agree with you. I don't think Duff is dead."

He waited for a minute, then said, "You mean my scenario—"

"Your scenario is entirely reasonable. Much more so than mine. In fact, I don't even have one."

"But if Duff is alive anywhere in this world, short of being insane or incarcerated, she knows what's happened and she—"

"She'd never allow it to go on. Say no more. That's where my whole theory breaks down—if it can be called a theory. Hand me that twistum, please."

I secured the trash, pushed a couple of chairs back in place, then sat down and looked at Brimmer. He hadn't moved. He was standing with his hands in his pockets, staring at the floor.

"There's one way you could help Louise immeasurably," I said. "Take your daughter off her hands—for a few weeks at least."

"Yes, that occurred to me." He moved, the picture of miserable uncertainty. "It's just that . . . well, it's been so long. I might handle the thing badly. The child might not even like me."

"Believe me, she'll like you fine."

"I thought maybe a camp would—"

"No! For God's sake, don't send her to camp!"

Why was I practically shouting? I got out of my chair and faced him.

"Mr. Brimmer, I know you have a schedule that would kill a horse. You're busy and sought after and on the go. But here's what you should do: For the next thirty days take your daughter with you everywhere you go—*drag* her with you— studios, restaurants, planes, hotels—*everywhere*. Half the time she'll probably worry you or exasperate you or embarrass you. Hang in. Don't buy her any presents, and don't try to entertain her. When you're at home, let her cook and make her read. Let her sit in the room with you while you work, and let her interrupt you with her chatter and drive you crazy. Chances are you'll be exhausted and bored, and the month will seem like forever. But it could be the best thing that ever happened in her life or maybe yours."

He was staring at me nonplussed.

I went back to my chair and said lamely, "Excuse the tirade. I was sent to Woolcott Academy when I was thirteen. I never knew my father, but I had an elderly uncle who came sometimes and took me out to lunch and the movies. In my entire life I don't remember anything quite like it for happiness."

The utter heck with it. I was weary and unnerved and longing for Cape Cod. Brimmer was still standing wordlessly. Was that the sound of applause from outside? I went to the window. "The bishop's address was certainly brief. I congratulate him—or else—" As I looked, the clerical gentleman was assisted off the dais and was now being escorted in our direction. The poor man's predicament struck my apparently overwrought funny bone, and I sank into the desk chair in a fit of giggles.

Now Brimmer's wordless stare became one of near alarm.

I pulled myself together and said, "Okay, let's be practical. Louise will be coming in here shortly, and it's our job to give her some sense of security and support—God knows how—before we go."

He moved now. "When are you leaving?"

"As soon as my daughter can come get me."

"I should go too." Brimmer looked around the room almost absently. "I'm a mile deep in messages at the inn. But for some reason . . . I'm extraordinarily reluctant to leave."

Hmmmm.

He added, "I think I'll take a short walk."

Praise be. I felt the need to be alone again. Brimmer picked up the trash and went out.

I sat staring at the chair where Margo Llewelyn had sat three months ago and hornswoggled us into this morass. I set my mind on a replay of the conversation of that morning. Somewhere in it there must be a seed, a crumb, a hint, a foreshadowing . . . What had she talked about other than her children and her husbands? What names, places, events? I listed them on my fingers: the old days at Wooly, her mother's job there, her nonexistent father, her vacations with Louise, her summer job at St. Cecelia House, the detestable Frederika, Louise's widowhood . . . there was something else. Something to do with her present situation—got it! She was going to England—I heard her voice—"to do a cameo bit in a movie."

I was on my feet. No way could Violet have done that. She could stand in for Margo Llewelyn under almost any condition, but not before the camera. Either Duff had lied about the cameo appearance or—much more likely—she had never left this country.

I sat down, encouraged, and started over the list again. If one nugget had surfaced, perhaps another would. But when you count things, sheep, clues, whatever, you get drowsy. . . .

Thank goodness for the sound of voices in the foyer, or I'd have been caught with my mouth open and probably snoring. I heard something about the dinner and Louise was saying yes, she'd see them all later (I was struggling with my hair), and then there were introductions and the name Patrick Brimmer repeated in awe (was my dress straight?), and the door opened and Louise and Brimmer came in.

"Clara." She came straight to me and kissed me. "I can't believe you stayed. How can I thank you? Now you *must* go."

"Yes, I'm off. But Mr. Brimmer and I have been huddling"—I wasn't going to let him off the hook—"and he has something to tell you that will do wonders for your morale."

"What Mrs. Gamadge means"—Brimmer took Louise's cap and gown from her—"is that she's been lecturing me on my duties as a father, and I'm prepared to bite the bullet. But not without a toast to my new role. I'll be right back." He turned and went out again.

Louise looked at me in surprise. "What does he mean?"

"By 'a toast,' I can guess. By his 'duties as a father,' well, I'm afraid I sounded off."

She laughed and said simply, "He's rather terrific, isn't he?"

"He's terrific, and I think he's in love."

"Oh, stop. Twenty-four hours?" Then her expression changed. "Twenty-four hours. Has it really been such a short time since Celestra came screaming in here?"

"Not much more."

She kicked off her pumps and laid them beside the desk. "We'll go to the police after the dinner. . . ." She rubbed one instep, her face somber, "Harry thinks the worst that can happen is she'll be committed." Then, pathetically grateful, she added, "It's kind of him to wait till school closes, isn't it?"

"Yes, it is."

We sat in silence, then Louise said, "Has it really all happened, Clara? And worse, might something still be happening—if it is—and where?"

Easy to interpret this jumbled syntax. "Brimmer thinks Duff's dead."

The foot she was rubbing twitched slightly. "What . . . do you think?"

I hate an outright lie, but this one was wrung from me in mercy. "I think he's probably right, and we should lay the whole matter to rest after Celestra is convicted of killing Margo Llewelyn."

Brimmer came back in pulling a bottle of champagne from a paper bag. He smiled at Louise as she sat motionless holding her instep.

"Nice of you to provide a slipper, but I think there are still some glasses—yes, here we are." He set three on the desk and began pulling the foil from the top of the bottle. "I brought this back with lunch intending to leave it with you as a token of appreciation, but now I think we have something to celebrate. I am about to become a father. What do you say to this plan: I go get my daughter—wherever she is—and keep her for a month, or till she gets sick of me. As warranties say: whichever comes first."

He popped the cork, I said "Yeah!" and Louise looked up at

him delightedly. "You mean it? That's wonderful, just wonderful! Louise will be *thrilled*."

It was the first time I'd heard the child's name mentioned between them.

Brimmer said thoughtfully, "She's named for you, I gather."

"I gather."

"It's a pretty, old-timey name." He poured, handed us each a glass, and raised his own. "Shall we toast the two Louises?"

Louise smiled. "I was always 'Lou' to Duff. I never liked others to call me that, but from her I didn't mind. 'Lou, stop studying and come have fun!' Or 'Lou, I hate this stuck-up school!' Or . . . or . . . 'Lou, I want my girls . . . with you.' "

Her hand shook. I put my glass down and got to her as she went quite to pieces, breaking into gasping sobs. Brimmer grabbed her glass and stood mute, the glass in each hand tipping and spilling. I moved from Louise and took the glasses from him and set them on the desk, wiping them. When I turned, he was putting her down in a chair. Now he squatted beside it, his hands on the arms. Finally, he pulled a handkerchief from his pocket and laid it on her lap. He said, "It's used. Sorry."

Louise smiled and choked and blew her nose. She said, "I've done nothing but weep and wail since you two arrived. I'm a bore."

"Oh, I can top you there." Brimmer straightened up. "How's this for boring: may I bring Louise back here first?"

"But you must. I'll get her clothes ready." Louise applied the handkerchief to her eyes and blew her nose a final time. She stood up and slid into her pumps. "And she'll have to take care of her own clothes and be reminded to wash her hair. Can you bring in some nice woman friend to help in that department?" Looking daunted, Brimmer nodded. Louise was at her desk, scribbling. "Here's the address and phone. And I'll call and vouch for you. The girls are at St. Cecelia House, a music school in St. Albans, Vermont. I'm afraid it's way upstate. Near Burlington."

Rather dazedly, Brimmer took the slip of paper she handed him. I had a hard time keeping a straight face. Was the man wishing to heaven he'd never set foot in this place?

Then he surprised me by saying, "Tell me if I'm getting carried away: would you like me to bring the other two back with me?"

Louise beamed at him. "Mr. Brimmer, I didn't have the courage to ask you. Yes, that would be so great. I want to keep the girls together as much as possible. Thank you!"

"But I should warn you," he said, running his hand over his head, "that I'm not awfully good with kids. I hardly know my own, and I've never even seen the other two. They may not take to me. They may opt to stay up there."

Louise smiled and shook her head decidedly. I winked at her and said, "No such luck." That made them laugh, and I added, "If you two don't want your champagne, I'll drink all three."

Brimmer topped the glasses, and we each took one. We stood facing each other. He said, "Here's a toast straight from the heart. To Duff, who probably doesn't give a damn what's happened to her, because her kids are with her old pal."

Louise said, "Oh, Lord—amen, I guess." And I think I said, "Here, here," but I'm not sure, because my mind was suddenly gyrating. What had set it going? Was it just the champagne, or was it the wording of Brimmer's toast?

That evening I told my gyrating mind to *quit it till morning*.

Louise and Harry went to their dinner, Patrick Brimmer went home, and I went to bed. I'd called Paula and asked her pick me up and she said sure, but would tomorrow be okay? It was not only okay, it was better. After supper in the dining hall, I went gratefully back to the quiet Head's house where, without the kids, cats, and confusion of Paula's place, I fell instantly asleep.

I struggled awake as Louise's agitated voice penetrated the darkness. She and Harry had received an urgent call at the dinner. Celestra had disappeared.

13

The Monday morning sunlight poured in through the window, lighting up a large autographed picture of Tip O'Neill, the only ornamant on the desk of Chief Emmet Eagan of the Woolcott police. The big, gray-haired man sat looking at us in stunned disbelief.

We had asked for a private interview with him, and now the reason for it had hit him amidships. He stared at our three stricken faces.

"*Celestra? Celestra Riondo?* She goes to my church!"

Did the entire Woolcott police force go to Celestra's church?

Harry kept repeating, "My fault! My fault!"

Louise kept repeating, "Oh, the poor thing, the poor thing! Where is she?"

I kept repeating, "Will you two please let Chief Eagan get a word in edgewise?"

But the chief was doing his own repeating. "*Celestra?* How do you know?"

We'd agreed that Harry would do the talking, which he now

did, giving an account of Celestra's confession and our realization that despite its bizarre improbability, the prints on the knife would undoubtedly corroborate it when matched with hers.

But poor Harry interrupted his narrative with so much self-recrimination that I finally said, "Chief, Mr. Parr was just anxious to spare the school more ugly publicity till after closing. The delay in reporting to you was only going to be for a few hours, and Celestra *had* been admitted to the hospital and *was* under surveillance."

"Some surveillance," said Eagan grimly, and who could disagree? He picked up a piece of paper. "Have you been told how she got away?"

Three heads shook mutely. He pulled a pair of glasses from his shirt pocket.

"This is the nurse's report. She was pretty hysterical, but Dr. Metcalf takes the responsibility for allowing the patient to return to the school." He read:

> When graduation was over, the patient, Celestra Riondo, asked if she might go back to her room on the school grounds as she would like to make both of us a cup of tea. I phoned the doctor and asked permission to stay a while longer, and he said how did she seem, and I said fine. He said okay but be back at the hospital by six. After we had tea, the patient asked if she could lie down for a while because she felt tired, so I said she could. She was soon in what seemed like a heavy sleep. I went into the bathroom, where I remained for maybe three or four minutes. When I came out, the patient was gone and so was her car.

Eagan stopped reading but continued to look down at the paper. Obviously there was more. He cleared his throat and read on:

Naturally I was very upset and worried for fear of what might happen to the patient. She was so gentle and trusting and . . . harmless.

We sat in silence, then the chief said briskly, "Well, so far I have no evidence of anything except that Celestra Riondo is a missing person. Would you like to know what steps we've taken since she was reported so last night?"

Three mute nods. We'd run out of lamentations.

"Of course, descriptions of her, her car, and the license plate have gone out. We spoke to her pastor, and he hasn't seen Celestra since church last Sunday. We likewise drew a blank with such members of the school staff as remain on the premises. Everyone seems to think she had few friends in the area and her life revolved around Woolcott Academy. Can you verify that, Mrs. Littleton."

"Yes."

"What about friends elsewhere?"

"None that I know of." Louise looked horribly pale. "A few years ago she told me that her Christmas card to her one friend in Miami had been returned. The woman would have been elderly, so . . ." She stopped, defeated.

Eagan tapped his pencil, frowning. "I assume we can take fingerprints from her room, her office—wherever."

"Of course." Louise went, if possible, a little paler. "But wouldn't that arouse . . . ?"

"Suspicion of a crime? No. We usually do ask for prints of missing persons. Sometimes it's necessary for—er—identification."

What a ghastly thought. I couldn't look at my companions.

The chief added quickly, "Of course, there will be no comparing of her prints with those on the knife till I give the word."

This was a crumb of relief.

Harry said, "I'm told that sometimes people take off for no other reason than to be found."

"Yes, that happens. In fact, Celestra could be somewhere on the school grounds, just hiding."

The thought was half comforting and half appalling, and we were again speechless.

Eagan leaned forward and straightened the picture of Tip O'Neill. He said, looking at it, "From the way you describe her, she's a pretty sick woman. She could be sick enough to want to . . ."

Harry quietly finished for him. "To want to kill Margo Llewelyn's children to save them from the wicked world."

Speechless gave way to gasping. "Thank God, I sent them away!" Louise put her hands to her head.

"Did you?" Eagan nodded. "That's good."

"And her car *is* gone," I said desperately.

"Yes, that's a pretty good sign she's taken off."

The phone on the desk rang, and Eagan excused himself and talked. We sat looking at each other, frightened and mortified that our humane plot had backfired.

"I think we should go," Louise said uncertainly.

"I have another question," said Harry.

"So do I." The chief put down the receiver. "Who will represent Celestra if—when we find her?"

"I will," said Harry. "That is, I'll get somebody. I'm not in criminal law."

Louise looked at me. "Are your son and his wife?"

His wife! I jerked and looked at my watch. Tina could have arrived at the airport, been met by Paula, and they might this instant be pulling up before the Head's house! I said hastily, "No, they're not in criminal either—but Tina could be arriving right now, Louise. Shouldn't we—" I began to rise as I spoke.

"It's okay." She pulled me gently down. "I left word for her to come here and why."

And why. More explanations. Tina would know nothing about Celestra's disappearance. Her disappearance? Tina would know nothing about *Celestra*. Oh, dear, how much backing up we would have to do and always needing to tread carefully around the Duff matter. I tried to concentrate on Harry's question, which had to do with the procedure when—and if—Celestra was found.

Eagan said, "She'll be brought back to the hospital. Then if guilt is established, I'll go to the state attorney's office and ask for a sealed indictment. After that, it's up to her lawyer."

Again we just sat there. Then it occurred to me to say, "What if she's left the state?"

"Then the police of whatever state she's found in will be responsible for returning her here. But I think that's unlikely." The chief gave us a small, consoling smile. "My guess is that Celestra is driving around aimlessly waiting—maybe even hoping—to be picked up."

Harry stood up. "Thank you, Chief."

As we walked in the baking sun down the main street of Woolcott toward Harry's car, Louise said, "Should we tell Patrick Brimmer?"

"Let's not," I said. "What can he do?"

"And he must have a deluge of work to catch up on," said Harry. "He was interviewed on the early news this morning. He spoke very freely about the murder and how shocked he was.

"And he said some nice things about Margo Llewelyn." Louise's arm, linked in mine, tightened a little. "Some very nice things."

"I wish I'd heard him," I said.

"So we'll leave him alone." Harry took out his keys. "Let him have his peace of mind."

His peace of mind? Louise and I looked at each other. Oh, Harry, if you knew how little peace of mind Patrick Brimmer has or may ever have.

I said as we reached the car, "When is he coming up to get his daughter?"

"In a few days." Louise looked down the street. "He said he'd call me. I hope he doesn't back out."

"He won't."

"You mean," Harry said, looking delighted, "he's going to take the child?"

"For a month."

"It's a start," I said.

"Of course it is! That's splendid, Louise! You see, some good has come of this mess. I always say—"

"Mother!" It was a shout followed by two beeps on a horn.

Oh, blessed voice! Oh, blessed disheveled head of my son, Henry, sticking out of a car window, Tina beside him waving! I flew to them ignoring the perils of Main Street.

"Not both of you! *Both!* What have I done to deserve this?"

"Very little," said Henry. "We're mad at you for staying on here so long."

"We figured," said Tina, "it would take the full team to pry you loose."

"Come meet your clients." I pointed. "No—park down there, and we'll come to you."

I trotted back to Louise and Harry who stood smiling. "The Gamadge team," I said happily, and we walked three car lengths to where Henry was pulling in.

Introductions were a bit garbled because I kept interrupting to ask when they'd arrived, if they'd had lunch, how long they could stay, if they'd like to consult first with Louise, then with Harry, or with Harry, then with Louise, or perhaps—

"Mother," Henry said, rolling his eyes, "will you please stop quarterbacking this thing and get in the car? We're taking you back to Paula's. From there we'll call Mrs. Littleton and Mr. Parr and set up an appointment. Okay with you folks?"

Emphatic okays ensued from Louise and Harry. Squelched but happy, I started to climb in the back of Henry's car. I said, "But I have to go back to Wooly for my things."

"Do you know the way back there?" asked Tina.

"Sort of. I think you take the next left and then—"

"We'll tail you, Mr. Parr," called Henry.

It was a ten-minute ride, and I hung over the front seat clasping my son's shoulder with one hand and touching Tina's pretty black hair with the other.

"You've cut it," I said reproachfully.

"Too hot. Clara, they said at the school that somebody had 'gone missing,' as the Brits say. Who?"

Back to horrid reality. I said, "Louise's secretary. A Cuban woman. Very psychotic case. I'll tell you about it when we get to Paula's. Does she know we're coming?"

"Of course," said Henry. She's worried that you're overly involved. She offered to meet us at the airport, but we know she's working so we rented this car. Any further developments on the murder investigation?"

"Well, yes."

"Like what?"

"Like . . . we know who killed her."

Henry's brakes screamed, and a horn blared behind us.

"Damn it, Henry!" Tina leaned out of the window and called "Sorry!" She pulled her head in. "Not that I blame you!" They both glared back at me.

"My God, Mom, don't do that to me again! *We* know who killed her? Who the hell is 'we'?"

"Harry Parr and Louise and I. Now I'm going to shut up. And

don't say a word about this when we get to Wooly. It's superconfidential, and I'm trusting you absolutely."

I sat back suddenly tired, some of the happiness draining out of me.

Tina reached back with an anxious look and patted my hand. Henry said grimly, "It's a good thing we came. You're freaked, Mom."

Harry turned into the school grounds, now wonderfully quiet and nearly abandoned, and we pulled up behind him before the Head's house. In the office everybody exchanged cards, an appointment was made for the next morning, and within minutes Harry was gone and Louise was up the stairs ahead of me and into my room. We pulled clothes from the closet and exchanged just two sentences.

Me: Don't bother to fold stuff. I'm a sloppy packer.

Louise: You're not sloppy about anything, and I'll never, never forget what you've done for me.

We went downstairs. Henry took the bag, and Tina took my arm. I felt anchored; a little bit of that happiness began to seep back in.

14

So talk," said Henry.

I'd refused to till I'd guided him back to the interstate. Now we were on the ramp. I said plaintively, "Let me wait till we get to Paula's so I won't have to go through it twice."

"If you weren't my mother I'd kill you. TALK!"

Well, I talked, and it was tricky. I had never not leveled with my family before, and I felt miserably guilty. But the Duff matter was verboten, and Louise and Patrick Brimmer trusted me. So I picked my way around the abyss and landed on safe ground with Celestra's confession and disappearance, and Chief Eagan's summation.

They'd been completely silent. Henry hadn't interrupted once—unusual for him—and now Tina—unusual for her—was crying a little. As we slowed at the intersection of the Fall River Expressway, Henry said, "Is Celestra likely to kill herself in a fit of remorse?"

"No," said Tina at once, "that would be a worse sin in her

book, right, Clara?" I nodded. "I agree with the chief. She's hanging out somewhere nearby."

"She has to eat and sleep," said Henry.

"Sure, but she isn't dumb. She'd be safe pulling around back of a motel somewhere after dark. If she doesn't know many people . . ."

I let them talk, my mind on Duff. My mental gyrations, which had been set in motion yesterday, had been knocked on the head by the events of today. Now they revived with a vengeance, and I couldn't wait to get to a phone.

Henry was saying, "I suppose the chief will still have to go through the motions of an investigation."

"More than just motions," said Tina. "He has no concrete evidence yet." She turned in her seat. "Tell me about Margo's kids, Clara. How long will they have to stay up in that school in Vermont?"

I digressed happily on Patrick Brimmer's munificence, and it took us to within a few minutes of Paula's house and a Denny's.

"I'm hungry," said Henry, "and there will be nothing to eat at my sister's but peanut butter."

I wasn't hungry, but I hoped there would be a phone. There was, and on a trip to the restroom I was able to check the yellow pages for car rentals in Dedham.

An hour later we turned into Paula's driveway, avoiding a bicycle and the cats, and coming to rest in a pothole. No sign of the van.

"That's odd." I looked at my watch. "She's usually home by now."

Henry and Tina sat looking at the house. Henry said, "Did they by any chance buy this place from the Addams family?"

"Oh, I forgot," I said. "You two haven't seen it. It will be very nice when they get it fixed up."

"It's very nice right now," said Tina loyally. "I wonder where Paula is."

"Let's hope she's rushed out to get something other than peanut butter," said Henry. "Shall we go in?"

"Will it be unlocked?" asked Tina.

"Andy and Paula," I said, "don't know what a lock is." I spied a large piece of paper hanging beside the kitchen door. "Is that a note?"

"Yes," said Henry, "there does seem to be something flapping there besides the shingles." We alighted and went to the door, then stood looking at each other in dismay. The scrawl read, "Make yourselves at home, back soon, gone to airport."

"*Airport!*" gasped Tina. "But we distinctly told her that we'd—"

She got no farther. An unrelenting horn sounded from the end of the street all the way to the drive. The van careened in and discharged beaming Paula, yelping Janey and Andrea—and martyred-looking Sadd!

It was one of those reunions that are rendered enormously more fun by their unexpectedness. For the first ten minutes everybody talked at once, then Sadd bellowed that if we didn't shut up he'd demand to be driven back to the airport. No, he did *not* want to be "shown the house"; he wanted to be shown the refrigerator and a cold beer if there was such a thing. There was, and we stood in the kitchen drinking when another horn blared and Andy bounded in. More hugging, kissing, with cats scattering underfoot.

Finally, while the young people swarmed about from attic to cellar to yard, Sadd and I settled down in the den.

"I hope I'm not being pushy," he said, sipping his beer, his feet on a dilapidated hassock, "but Florida was getting hot, and I was dreaming of Cape Cod. Is the cottage available?"

"Of course." My thoughts were miles away. "It has been since June first. Avail yourself."

"What about you?"

"Well," I said bracing myself for the tirade, "I'm not going there right now."

"Clara"—here it came—"you're still cooking on this murder."

"I'm *not* cooking on the murder," I said truthfully. Then, anxious to change the subject, "Isn't this a great old house? They can do wonders with it."

"What's the matter?"

I was puzzled. "With the house?"

"With you."

There's no use playacting with Sadd. He's what's known in the antique trade as a "divvie." But he doesn't divine true treasures; he divines true feelings.

I said guardedly, "Well, there have been some new developments."

"Bad?"

"Sad."

"Having to do with the murder?"

"Yes. I'll tell you about it tonight with the others."

Sadd looked at me steadily. "Anything else?"

"My, aren't you the father confessor." Was the word "Duff" written in large letters on my forehead? "What else would there be?"

"Clara"—he took his feet from the hassock—"when the news of the murder broke, I tried to call you a dozen times but couldn't get through. So I called Paula, and she said, 'There's something worrying Mother besides the murder,' and I said, 'Of course there is—it's those children.' "

What a relief. I said, "Yes, they have been rather on my mind."

"Now, Clara"—Sadd reached for his beer—"I said it last winter, and I'll say it again: if you persist in agonizing about those kids . . ."

I let him preach on, so grateful was I for his supposition. Then I said, "Actually, it's all been rather happily settled. Margo Llewelyn's will names Louise Littleton as their guardian. Margo set it up before she went abroad."

Sadd's eyes widened. "How superb! I knew there was a reason I loved that woman apart from her gorgeousness. Have they a clue as to who killed her? Wait—I'm not certain of 'gorgeousness.' It's always risky to make an adjective into a noun. You run the danger . . ."

Again, I was grateful. Sadd's fanatical devotion to good grammar spared me having to talk till later. Cats, kids, and grandkids poured in from the backyard, and there was bedlam.

At ten o'clock that night moonlight drenched the front porch.

Sadd and I claimed the only two chairs, rickety though they were, and the young people sprawled about on the floor and steps. Janey and Andrea had been batted back to bed half a dozen times and had finally stayed put. I was on.

In that silvery glow, the tragedy of Celestra sounded, to me at least, even more poignant. Nobody spoke as I finished; there were only little sounds of dismay and compassion.

Then Sadd said, "It's right out of Valaire's 'Les Femmes Perdu.' "

No one could ever comment on Sadd's obscure references, and Paula said, "The person I feel sorriest for is Louise."

Murmurs of assent.

Andy said, "How long has Celestra been gone?"

I thought back. "Since late yesterday afternoon."

"She's got to have left town."

"But where would she go?" Henry, lying on his back, came to a sitting position. "Mrs. Littleton says she doesn't know anybody."

"Now, I consider that an unfounded statement." Sadd adjusted himself in the creaking chair. "Surely the woman had days off, took vacations. How could anyone be certain she didn't have friends elsewhere?"

This sounded reasonable, and we sat and mulled it for a few seconds.

Then Tina said suddenly, "They might find the car without her."

The thought of that little car, its bumper declaring that God loves you, sitting abandoned on some byway chilled and saddened me. And why had Sadd's remark started mental gyrations of another kind? I got up stiffly.

"Good night, all. Where do I sleep, dear?"

"Same room, Mom." Paula jumped up. "I've got futons for everybody else."

"Futons!" Sadd's voice rang with horror.

"Not for you, Sadd." She kissed him. "You're in the den. The sofa pulls out."

"Then so do I, tomorrow," Sadd said to me as we went inside. "One night on anything that 'pulls out' is enough. Dammit, Clara, I wish you'd come on down to the Cape with me. Can you give me one good reason—"

"Yes, I can." A convenient fib had just occurred to me. I took the stuff Paula was dragging from a chest in the den and told her I'd make up the bed.

"Thanks, Mom. Good night. We'll probably hang out for a while."

Extraordinary to me, no doubt because I'm old, is the ability of the young to "hang out" indefinitely. I was dropping. I tossed some sheets on the lumpy pull-out for Sadd and said to him, "I'll follow you down to the Cape soon, but since I'm here, I plan to spend a few days with a friend in the area." I kissed him. "Sleep tight."

"Ha!"

I went up the stairs and at the top I hesitated, then walked into Paula and Andy's room and stood looking at the phone. The clock radio said 11:30, but I doubted that Louise Littleton was sleeping much these days.

She answered at once.

"Louise, it's Clara."

"Clara! Is it wonderful being with your family?"

"Yes, wonderful. Any word?"

"No. Chief Eagan said the search is going New England–wide tomorrow."

"Louise"—I swallowed—"did you ever—I mean—does Celestra know of . . . the existence of St. Cecelia's?"

Silence. Then I heard—or did I feel?—Louise also swallow. She said, "Yes. I correspond with Sister Beranice."

"But Celestra doesn't know the children have been sent there."

"No. No, she doesn't know that."

"But if she's gone there for . . . for spiritual guidance, she might see them."

"Yes, she might." Louise's voice had grown fainter and fainter. Now she rallied. "I'll call Chief Eagan this minute."

"Wouldn't it be better to call Sister Beranice first?"

"Of course. What's the matter with me." She'd begun to sound short of breath.

"I could be wrong, wrong, wrong."

"Shall I call you back?"

"No. It's late. And I don't think I want to know."

"I don't blame you."

"But I'll see you tomorrow. I'm planning to—er—visit a friend in the area, so I'll come down with Henry and Tina. By then you'll know."

"Oh, God, maybe the world will know."

I hung up and went to bed with Chief Eagan's words ringing in my ears. *"She could be sick enough to want to kill Margo Llewelyn's children to save them from the wicked world."*

15

The next morning, with Paula, Andy, and the girls gone, we sat over a second round of coffee and I decided against renting the car in Dedham. Only fair to see Louise once more. Suppose Celestra . . . I'd pick up a car in Woolcott for my proposed jaunt, even though I now felt like singing with Nathan Detroit, *"Talk about your long shot!"*

"What time is your appointment with Louise and Harry?" I asked.

"Ten." Henry looked at his watch. "We should leave."

"Is it at Wooly?"

"Yes."

"May Sadd and I bum a lift with you? I'd like to see Louise once more."

"Sure," said Tina. "Then are you going on to the Cape?"

"Sadd is. I'm going to visit a friend in the area (that amorphous friend!) so Sadd can take you to the airport and use your rental car to go on down to Chatham."

I'd worked hard at this scenario and thought it sounded casual and reasonable. But Henry and Tina looked at me suspiciously.

"What friend?" said Henry.

I was ready for that. "Nobody you ever knew. I grew up with her. She lives in Newton." There was such a person, I told my twitching conscience. I added querulously, "I think I've earned a change and a little distraction after all this."

Indisputable, and other than Sadd complaining that I was disposing of him in a rather summary fashion, they let me alone. Quite pleased with myself, I went up to my room, threw nightgown and toothbrush back in the bag, and started down the stairs. Three steps from the bottom I heard it.

". . . self-confessed killer of Margo Llewelyn . . ." The TV in the den blared. ". . . small Vermont town . . ." I sat down on the step and covered my ears. Tina turned, saw me, said "Henry, shut it off," and ran to me.

I said, "No, go ahead and listen. I just can't."

"It can wait." Henry shut the thing off, and they came and stood around me. Sadd patted my hand, said "There's a Latin proverb," and quoted something that I took to be comforting.

Tina said, "Did you even remotely consider St. Cecelia's?"

"Well . . . remotely."

Henry was gazing at me thoughtfully. "I wonder who tipped them off."

I stood up. "I'm sure Louise will know. Let's go."

We drove down to Woolcott without saying much. I was pretty shattered, but with distress came a certain relief. It was over. Celestra would be in good hands, and she was out of my life. But Duff wasn't. Would she ever be? At one point Sadd said, "I wish you'd change your mind and come to the Cape," and I nearly agreed to. Then I realized that the gyrations would continue to gyrate—an extremely wearing sensation—unless I silenced them. Henry refrained from turning on the car radio, for which I thanked him as we neared the school grounds.

Poor Wooly! Again it swarmed with gloating media, but faithful officer Jim was at the Head's house to usher us in. And poor Louise and poor Harry! They were waiting for us with strained faces. I introduced Sadd, who tactfully said he had seen that glorious word "Library" over one of the school buildings and would wait there till business was done.

Almost at once, Louise said, "Mr. Parr, will you tell Henry and Tina how it all happened? I want to ask Clara something."

She clutched my arm and pulled me toward the stairs. We went halfway up and sat down.

I said, "First, how about telling *me* what happened?"

She nodded and ran her fingers through her hair. She looked drawn but young and pretty in a summer dress.

"I called St. Cecelia's immediately, and Sister Beranice said yes, a woman named Celestra Riondo had arrived a few hours ago in a troubled condition. Sister recognized the name from our correspondence, and she asked Celestra if I knew she was there. Celestra said no, nobody knew, that she'd come alone because she needed a quiet place to think and pray."

Louise was trembling. I put my hand over hers and suddenly saw, in a sad flashback, hers over Celestra's, only three nights ago.

"Of course, Sister realized the poor thing was disturbed and exhausted—she'd been eating and sleeping in her car—and what she needed most was rest and counseling. She had her put to bed and made an appointment with the doctor to see her. She was just about to pick up the phone to call me when I called her."

I said, "That poor Sister! What a blow."

"Clara, she handled it so well. I had to tell her the whole story and say—even though it killed me—'Don't let her near Margo Llewelyn's children.' She just said, 'What do you want me to do?'

and I said to ask Mr. and Mrs. Manetti to stand by till the police arrived, then come back with Celestra. Then I called Chief Eagan."

"Had he been here to take her fingerprints?"

"Yes."

I stared down at Louise's foot moving restlessly on the step. "He moved fast."

"The Vermont police had her back here at the hospital by two this morning. The Manettis said she mostly slept in the police car but woke up when she saw Chief Eagan and smiled at him. He told me she answered all his questions as if she was glad to, almost as if—"

"No more, no more." I squeezed her hand and stood up.

Louise didn't. She said, "Patrick Brimmer called me this morning. He'd just heard. Of course he was flabbergasted, but he said we should be grateful it was out of our hands."

"He's right. You said you wanted to ask me something."

"Yes—er—are you going on down to the Cape now?"

I was tempted to share my gyrations with her, but it seemed as if Louise had had enough for the time being, so I trotted out the tired tale of my friend in Newton. She looked pleased.

"Really? That makes it easier to ask what I'm going to ask."

Damn. Was my fib going to get me in hot water?

"Patrick is going up to St. Cecelia's to get the girls day after tomorrow. He asked me to go with him, but I feel I should be here for Celestra. Will you go, Clara? I mean meet him up there and help break the ice and so forth? The girls know you from their stay with your family—and I'm sure he'd appreciate it. I have a nerve asking you, but since you're going to be in this area . . ."

Well, I'd asked for it. Bridgeport, Connecticut—my real destination—was about as "in this area" as it was in the area of the moon; but I'd been blabby and now I was stuck.

I said reluctantly, "Day after tomorrow? That's Thursday. Well . . . okay."

She hugged me, and we went back to the others. I said at once, frantic to get away, "May I be selfish and grab your car, Henry? Would it be very difficult to get another rental?"

Henry smiled as he handed me the keys. "Mr. Parr has been filling us in. So you only thought 'remotely' of St. Cecelia's."

I felt uncomfortable. "Sister was about to call Louise anyway. Well, get to your business."

Harry embraced me and said he and his wife had a place in Orleans on the Cape, and would come see me. Louise and Tina walked out to the car with me. Louise said, "Have a nice, relaxing visit," and Tina called as I pulled away, "Where can we reach you in Newton?" but I pretended not to hear and set out for my nice, relaxing visit.

Route 95 south through Rhode Island and into Connecticut was not congested on that June weekday. The sun shone, and I drove slowly, allowing myself to cogitate thus:

Margo Llewelyn and Violet La Grange strike a bargain. Margo is in need of R and R—anonymously—and Violet is in need of money. Margo says Vi, here's all my identification and cards. Go to England for three months, be me, and use them freely. Cancel the movie bit—I'm known for my erratic cancellations—be seen here and there in dark glasses, fleetingly, and "this is where the kids are" (Patrick Brimmer's words). Never write to them, just send presents and two thousand dollars at Easter. Meanwhile, your sister in Bridgeport, who also needs money, will house me— I'll wear a black wig—and help me get back on my feet. In June, you richer and I restored, we swap back.

But they hadn't figured on Celestra.

New London, Connecticut. Exits jammed. Mystic Seaport big

at this time of year. . . . But what had taken Violet to Woolcott Academy? Patrick Brimmer's theory didn't fit with mine.

New Haven. More jammed exits. Graduation at Yale? Had Duff, perhaps not better at all, but in fact, very, very much worse, implored Violet to bring her children to her? I tried to envision the panic of Violet's sister when news of the murder broke. She was trapped now with a frightful burden whom she perhaps had to restrain or, equally awful, an inert creature, uncaring and totally dependent.

Bridgeport, Connecticut. Not exactly a center of elegance, I thought, as I traversed dingy, trash-strewn streets and brought the car to a stop before a gas station. A mutilated phone book yielded the addresses of the two La Granges; I prayed they would be near neighbors. They were not. An attendant, looking at what I had written down, said that "one of them streets was a dump over near the ferry." The other was "more residential." I opted for residential, and he gave me excellent directions.

There are residences and residences. The one I found at 6 South Vine Street was a "three decker" depressingly in need of repair. Even a broom would have helped. Not an inch of parking space on the street. "Heaps," as my son calls them, lined both sides. I hesitated, then turned my car into the narrow, cracked cement driveway of number 6. I sat for a moment, certain that if I was infringing, a head would appear at a window and a voice would order me off. No head, no voice.

I got out, locked the car—hoping it would survive the neighborhood—and looked up at the peeling structure. Absolutely ideal quarters for a celebrated person boarding incognito.

I walked up the worn steps, climbed over a broken scooter, and looked in vain for a doorbell. The door was half wood, half ugly, tinted glass, saggily curtained. I tapped on the glass with my car keys.

A bedraggled but very pretty little girl opened the door. I said, falling into the classic saleman's lingo—but what other was there?—"Hello. Is your mother at home?"

"She doesn't live here."

"Oh. Who takes care of you?"

"My aunt. She's asleep."

"What's your name, dear?"

"Debbie."

"Debbie, does anyone else live here besides you and your aunt?"

"My other aunt. The sick one. But she can't come out of her room because she runs out in the street in her nightgown."

I swallowed and said to this aunt-ridden child, "Debbie, do you also have an Aunt Violet?" A nod. "Will you go tell your aunt—the one who *can* come out of her room—that she might like to see me because—"

"Who is it, Deb?" Muffled and from afar.

"A lady wants to know about Aunt Vi."

There were thudding footsteps. A door off the dark hall that stretched behind Debbie opened, and a very stout, fiftyish woman in a muumuu stood staring at me.

"My name is Clara Gamadge," I said. "I don't know yours— I'm sorry—but Violet's name being La Grange, I was able—"

"Kincaid. What about Violet? Are you the party that called me? No, that was a man. What about her?"

"May I come in, Mrs. Kincaid?"

She jerked her head toward an arch across the hall from where she stood. The little girl—she was really quite adorable—took my hand and walked with me into a room of indescribable dreariness. The child sat down on the hideous sofa and patted the spot beside her. I sat down there. Mrs. Kincaid lumbered after us.

"So what about Violet?" Her voice was harsh and shaky.

"Well, I was hoping you'd tell *me* about her. Let me explain: I don't know Violet, but I did know Margo Llewelyn—and wasn't that a terrible crime?" No response, just the stare. "I have friends who do know Violet, and they're worried about her because she seems to have more or less disappeared."

I'd put a lot of buzzwords into that speech, and they had the desired effect. Mrs. Kincaid moved unsteadily to a chair and got into it. She said thickly, "I'm worried sick. Three months ago she tells me to take her calls, say I'm her but I can't talk, and hang up. She gives me money and says there'll be more when she comes back. *Three months ago.* Where in hell is she?"

I shook my head sympathetically, and she complained on.

"A month ago my other sister dumped this one on me"—she waved a fat foot toward Debbie—"because she wanted to work, but what she pays me is a joke."

Another commiserating nod, and I said, "And Debbie says you have an elderly aunt living with you."

"Yeah, and she can't be left two minutes—besides the expense." Mrs. Kincaid scowled nervously. "I'm in a mess."

How much of a mess, I wondered, and was she in it alone? There was no mention of a Mr. Kincaid.

"Yes, the elderly can be such a burden," I said. Then for good measure, "And young children do tie you down." I patted the little hand beside me in mute apology. "Is your aunt able to get around?"

"No, she never leaves the room. I can't trust her. She takes off." Pause. "So you don't know nothing about Violet neither?" She surveyed me blankly. "This guy that phones me the other day, he said he seen her, but he hung up real fast and I think he was lying. I bet she's in trouble or . . . or"—she squared, as much as it's possible to square very round shoulders—"or let's face it. Maybe she's dead."

So we faced it and faced each other. Mrs. Kincaid's countenance glistened with perspiration, and mine might at any minute, not only because the room was stifling but because I felt

I was being dismissed. So I didn't stand up but sat frowning as if about to contribute something weighty.

Debbie scrambled off the sofa and said, "I'm going to see Auntie."

"Okay, but watch it." Mrs. Kincaid looked at me. "She can hit you if she's a mind to."

The child ran out and I said, "Your aunt likes children?"

"She likes this one."

Christine's age. My hostess stood looking at her lingering guest, who now did stand up and say, "Do you own this house, Mrs. Kincaid?"

"No. It's Vi's."

"Does she have a will?"

"Who knows?"

"Because," I plowed on desperate to provoke an outburst, "if she has a will and she's dead, she might have left it to you considering—"

"That's the whole goddam trouble!" I was getting my outburst. "What good does anything do me when I can't prove if she's alive or dead? When I can't prove a damn thing?"

How right she was. I said, "Yes, you are in rather a bind, aren't you?"

She was back in the hall now, and I no choice but to follow. I looked longingly down the narrow passage with its tantalizingly closed doors and glimpse of grubby kitchen at the end. I said, "You know, Mrs. Kincaid, I've had dealings with a lot of elderly people—heavens, I'm elderly myself!—and they interest me. I'd like to see your aunt."

The woman looked distraught. "No way. I'd be embarrassed. She's batty."

"All the more reason." I opened my pocketbook. "A visitor very often has a quieting effect"—where did I get that gem?—"and I do want to leave you a little gift"—I extracted my checkbook—"because I can see you've been through a lot." I was scribbling—make it enough, Clara, to allow you just a peek at Auntie. "And, as I said, I have great compassion for the elderly. After all"—rueful laugh—"I may be headed for 'batty' any day now—one never knows, does one? I would so like to see—er—meet your aunt."

I handed her the check, and her eyes zoomed to the amount. I'd gagged as I wrote two hundred, but I had to be sure of getting in. There was the almost audible clicking of Mrs. K.'s brain, then she said, "Let me see if she's—well, you know—"

"Presentable? Of course."

"I mean, I never know how I'll find her."

"I understand."

I stepped back, and she moved, slippers slapping, down to the door just before the kitchen. I stood still, envisioning the procedure: a pulling of the shade, a twitch of the wig, a threat to the occupant . . . The door opened, and Debbie looked out.

"Come on in, lady."

My feet suddenly felt rooted to the ground. I pried them up and walked down the hall to where the child was holding out her hand to me.

The room wasn't dark; in fact, sunlight poured in on its shabbiness and disorder. A lopsided bed stood against the wall, and beside it was a reeking commode. I advanced with fixed smile toward the crone in the dilapitated chair.

She was no more Margo Llewelyn or Elaine Duffy than I was.

16

Disappointment or relief? A chunk of both, and an even larger chunk of mortification and chagrin. Add a dash of pity, and you have my mental state as I sat on the splintery front steps of the house between Mrs. Kincaid clutching her check, and Debbie clutching a ten-dollar bill I'd given her. What is there about money, I wondered dully, that seems to unlock people? Debbie was listing her potential purchases, and Mrs. K. her grievances against Violet.

I was exhausted, bored, and longing to get away, but I sat, listening and nodding, between my pair of beneficiaries. To the little one on my left, I felt like saying, "What errant gene brightens you, and how soon will it be smothered?" and to the large one on my right, "Forget Violet. She killed her friend, got killed herself for her pains, and indirectly you helped with the crimes, so shut up."

Finally, I did stand up, brushed the grit from my backside, and said, "Your aunt looks very frail, Mrs. Kincaid. I don't think it can be too much longer."

"Sure it can. Her type live forever."

The whiny reply made it easier for me to hold out my hand and say good-bye. Debbie followed me to the car. I kissed her, unlocked the door, and got in. The day had grown warm, and the car was suffocating. I let down the window, backed into the street, and drove to the corner. Should I turn left or right? Appallingly, it didn't matter. I had no idea where I was or wanted to go. Turn left for loony, right for ridiculous. Loony brought me, in about three blocks, to a Burger King. I pulled in, parked, and sat looking at the word "Whopper." That's it, Clara, that describes your mistake. So much for your inspired scenario. Why didn't you listen to Patrick Brimmer. "Oh, Duff's dead." Sure she was.

But dead where? I stared at a "Thick Shakes" sign. And unavenged—that was the galling part. If only something or someone could shed a ray . . . I gave myself a mental shake, realizing my overactive mind had made me look dumb enough. The thing was over.

I rolled up the window, started the car, and turned on the air conditioner. Cape Cod. A great place to lick wounds. I could be in Chatham before dark. Sadd might even be there ahead of me. We'd go out to dinner. Nobody on earth would ever know I'd been a stupid ass. Tomorrow—

A horn blasted at me as I hit my brake. My promise to Louise! I jerked back into a parking place. Why, *why* had I said I'd go to St. Cecelia's? St. Albans, Vermont! It sounded like the end of the earth. I sat fuming, thinking of Tina's words, *"You don't owe Margo Llewelyn one more bloody damn thing."*

But a promise is a promise. I told myself to calm down and sat thinking. Perhaps the disturbing, three-way link between Louise and Patrick Brimmer and me called for some kind of resolution or even . . . benediction. Mightn't our tragic secret be somehow blessed and condoned—in my eyes at least—if I did see Duff's children once more and helped ease them into their new life? My! How virtuous I sounded, and how rather hypocritical. I suddenly realized I had another reason for going to Vermont.

I wanted to talk to those children.

I spent the night in a fleabag in Bridgeport.

Too tired to start the drive back, I'd pulled into "Ferry Rest" six blocks from the Burger King. It had a murky little dining room, and I put some salad on a paper plate and took it to my room, which cost thirty-nine dollars with a senior citizen discount. The sheets were reasonably clean, and the promised "rest" I took to mean that the traffic roar was definitely lower between the hours of one and four in the morning. It didn't matter. I lay awake thinking of how children tend to blab things about their parents and their parents' friends. It seemed likely that Duff's girls had known Violet—perhaps even well enough to have known some of her friends. Was it possible that Violet had had another accomplice, someone more informed and less complaisant than her sister? Might the children have . . . I wondered if the expression "little pitchers have big ears" was still in use.

What day was today? What time? My watch said Tuesday, June 5, 6:00 A.M.

Daylight was just glimmering, and the manager was making coffee (I instantly forgave him his sheets) as I came through the lobby. He proffered "nondairy creamer" in a paper cup, but the foreign specks in it made me decline. I asked for directions to Route 95 and took my not-bad-at-all black brew out to the car. It was the "misty moisty" morning of the nursery rhyme, and I sat sipping and staring at the procession of trucks.

A picnic might be nice. I could be at the Boston airport before noon, return the car, and get a flight to Burlington. Brimmer would not be going up until tomorrow. Surely Sister would let me take the children on a picnic supper this evening. Then either I'd be invited to stay over, or I'd grin and bear one more night at a motel. Tomorrow Brimmer and I would converge. I was undecided whether to tell him what, if any, information I might by then have gleaned from the children.

I started the car. Was it callous of me to think of pumping the poor, bereaved tykes even ever so chattily and indirectly? Well, it was in the cause of justice and, of course only incidentally, in the cause of Clara's insatiable curiosity.

Flights from Boston to Burlington, Vermont, are not exactly every hour on the hour. It was an excruciating four-hour wait during which I longed for human contact and didn't dare make any. I looked at the bank of phones and could hear the voices of my family. Where are you? What on earth are you doing *there?* I couldn't even call Louise. How would I answer her questions about my friend in Newton and whether I was enjoying my visit.

I wandered in and out of those mind-numbing shops in the airport, then bought a book of crossword puzzles and a Bloody Mary, and finally sat, stupified and waiting, my mind a blank.

And of course the plane was delayed taking off. What else?

I'd begun to think I was being punished for my insane persistence till I walked out of the Burlington airport and hailed a cab. Punished? The opposite. Vermont in June was a reward in itself, a leafy, twilight green paradise. But it was too late for a picnic supper. It would have to be a picnic breakfast. The cab driver knew a nice place to put up for the night, right in St. Albans. Sure he knew St. Cecelia's. His aunt used to work there.

From a charming room, Lake Champlain glimmering in the

distance, I called the school. A pleasant voice said yes, I was expected, and Mr. Brimmer was arriving tomorrow. The children would be ready. I'd be there quite early? Not a problem. A picnic breakfast? Delightful, but please, not before eight. Morning Song was at half past seven.

I ran a tub and lay in it exhausted, almost hoping I would draw a blank with Duff's children tomorrow. I half decided to abandon any form of questioning at all. My ludicrous miscalculation of yesterday was doing a belated job on me. What could you really do, Clara, with the random comments of three bewildered kids? But suppose . . . suppose . . .

The phone rang. Manifestly impossible. Not a soul in the world knew where I was. Somebody wanting somebody in another room. I ignored the ringing, and it stopped. I climbed out of the tub thinking I should probably eat for I hadn't since a sandwich at the airport. But I was almost too weary and depressed to stir.

The phone rang again.

Dammit. I picked it up. "You have the wrong room. This is number—"

"Mrs. Gamadge, it's Patrick Brimmer."

Impossible repeating itself. I was speechless.

He went on, "I'm in a room down the hall. I was surprised to see your name on the register. May I see you? I could come—"

"No, Mr. Brimmer, you may not see me or come, and you're not supposed to be here till tomorrow."

"Neither are you, for that matter." It was blunt and funny, and I began to laugh, albeit weakly. "But, by the way, thank you for coming at all. I thought I'd get over to the school rather early tomorrow. The drive back is longish."

"You haven't been to St. Cecelia's yet?" The man was ruining my plan.

"No. I just got here. In fact, now that you've arrived, what do you say to picking up those kids tonight and making a start back? We could stop over halfway down and—"

"Mr. Brimmer." I was cursing my fate. "I'm exhausted."

"Oh, of course. I'm sorry."

"And as for getting to the school early"—I had to either tip my hand or throw it in—"I plan to do just that, but I'm going to ask you not to come before ten, and not to ask me why."

After a long pause he said quietly, "You're up to something."

"Something so far-fetched that you won't get a word out of me now or ever unless . . ."

"Unless you pull off a coup."

The word jarred. "Not a coup—oh, God—not a coup!"

"Forgive me. Wrong word. Don't cry." Was I? Probably. Fatigue, frustration, and hunger were getting to me.

Brimmer said, "Forget everything I've said. Go to bed. Wait—have you eaten?"

"No, but—"

"Let me take you—"

"No. Thank you. No."

"In that case you'll find something at your door in half an hour. But if I feed you, and I agree about tomorrow, I deserve a crumb."

I said nothing.

"A crumb—in absolute confidence of course." I heard him draw a breath. "Does this far-fetched matter have to do with Duff's death?"

"Yes."

"You've found out something?"

"Nothing. I've found out nothing."

"But you might—"

"Good night."

"Just one more question. What do you like on your hamburger?"

A taxi took me through the golden haze of the next morning out to St. Cecelia House. On the way we stopped at a convenience store, and I picked up a carton of orange juice and a box of doughnuts. It was a quarter to eight when we turned into a weedy drive that ended at some attractive, rustic buildings breathtakingly surrounded by birch trees. The driver asked if I wanted to be picked up later; I said no, and he drove away.

Those birches. They were all over the place, glistening in the sun. From a grove of them came the sound of young voices raised in song. Almost too heavenly a setting, I thought grimly, for my rather obdurate intentions.

The word "Office" was scratched on a piece of birch over the door of the first building. I started toward it, then, on an impulse, changed course and walked in the direction of the grove. The music swelled distractingly, but I wasn't there to listen. I was looking for Margo Llewelyn's daughters.

There were about twenty children seated on benches, some with songbooks, some without, all following the waving arms of a young man in T-shirt and jeans. I stood a little distance away and searched each row.

Louise and Karen were seated together, looking about them at the faces of the singers. Where was Christine? No sign of her. Too young for matins? But there were others her age. Please don't let her be sick or rebellious or—I moved a step—there she was, asleep on a bench, her head on the lap of a warbling teenager.

The lovely chorus stopped on the dot of the young man's waving arms. He said something about the next hymn, and pages of songbooks rustled. I thought: Patrick Brimmer will come, and we'll take these wanderers back to the real world. But could there have been a lovelier interlude than this? Then I was angry with myself—attributing glory to just another bewildering episode in a chain of bewildering episodes. Don't be sentimental, Clara. Who knows what kids like? They may hate it here.

And the orange juice was getting heavy.

I walked back to the office door and knocked. A quavering voice said, "Coming!" and presently the door opened and a very old nun stood there. She said, "Good morning. You must be Mrs. Gamadge."

"Yes. Good morning, Sister."

"Come in. I'm Sister Beranice. Is Mr. Brimmer with you?"

"No, I came a little early because—"

"Of course . . . the picnic." She took the plastic bag from me. "What a nice idea. I don't believe I've ever heard of a picnic *breakfast*."

"Neither have I. I feel a little foolish. It's just doughnuts and juice."

"They'll love it, poor little things. They seem rather lost. I'm sure you've heard about the sad business of Celestra Riondo." I nodded. "Too dreadful for words. Would you like some coffee, Mrs. Gamadge?"

"Oh, would I. By the way, Louise said you handled the whole thing beautifully."

"I handled it with my heart in my mouth, I assure you. Do sit down." She went to an urn in a corner of the shabby, comfortable room. "Our main fear was that the children would find out Celestra was here. Fortunately she arrived after dark. I'll have a cup with you. Cream and sugar?"

"Just cream. And please take a doughnut. I imagine the press descended on you yesterday."

" 'Descended' is the word! But we'd anticipated that. We sent our three visitors and a few of the other children out for a day on the lake. One of our nice fathers has a boat." She handed me a mug and smiled down into the doughnut box. "Cinnamon! My favorite."

"Sister, I think you're a wonder."

She shrugged and sipped her coffee. "We all feel very sorry for those little girls. Did you know their poor mother?"

"No. She was Louise's friend back in their school days."

"So Louise said. Of course I know very little about the movies, but even I"—she laughed a little—"have heard of Margo Llewelyn."

My next sentence began with the words "I wonder if" and was to have continued with "anyone at St. Cecelia's knows that Margo Llewelyn used to work here in the summers." But I stopped, frozen.

"If what, my dear?" Sister was munching her doughnut.

But I could only sit staring at her, bereft of words.

Again, politely, "If what?"

"If by chance"—I put my coffee down and made a huge effort to keep my voice casual—"an old friend of Louise's and mine is here. She's been ill and in need of care, and she said she might—"

"You mean Miss Duffy?" The lined old face broke into a delighted smile. "Indeed she's here. Would you like to see her? Oh, I *am* pleased. You'll be her first visitor!"

17

The letter was difficult to write because, above all, I wanted to catch her voice.

I'd said to her, "Try not to talk so fast," and she did slow down—involuntarily toward the end; she was very weak, and death was less than a month away. But the old, volatile, maddening, endearing Duff was present in every word.

Louise, Patrick Brimmer, and I were sitting in the exact chairs we'd occupied five nights ago when, in dismay, doubt, and dread, we'd forged our bond. But now sunlight poured through the office window, and the shouts of Margo Llewelyn's children and others—it was the opening day of summer session—came to us distantly from the pool.

Louise said, "Will one of you read it to me? My glasses are upstairs."

I extended the letter to Brimmer, but he shook his head. "You'll understand your own handwriting better."

Valid as both statements may have been, I sensed that neither of my companions could bear to look at it. Sister Beranice had given me some sheets of paper, and I'd scrawled on them, thinking numbly that I'd copy this over later, but I knew I wouldn't, and I didn't, and the letter hadn't left my handbag since I'd folded it with its torrent of words and kissed Duff good-bye.

I spread the crumpled sheets on my knees, and they crackled in the quiet room. Would my voice hold up throughout? I wondered, and I read:

My dear, wonderful Lou,

Can you forgive me?

Mrs. Gamadge says that's the way I must start, or she won't write this letter for me. Okay, but she has to promise me something—that she'll put down everything I say even when it's something nice about her. And the first nice thing is this: she wouldn't let Patrick see me. I'd have *died*. You can't believe what a sight I am. Hey, that's funny, saying I'd have died when I'm dying anyway.

But oh, Lou, do you know what you did for me when you sent my kids here? At first I was terrified. Sister said Margo Llewelyn's children were coming, and I nearly panicked. Then I realized how smart you were to do it. I'm never out of my room now, and I could look out the window and see them playing. I'd sit there and watch them and bawl and bless you. I never, *never* expected to see them again, and it was like some kind of bloody miracle, and you were the one who—okay, Mrs. Gamadge says we'll both be crying in a minute so I better get on with it.

But how could *I* get on with it when my eyes were streaming, Louise was weeping quietly, and Brimmer was sitting with his face in his hands? I wiped my glasses, peered down at the letter, and found my place.

Of course you couldn't know, Lou, that when I walked into your office three months ago I was dying. The doctor had said maybe six months, maybe less and it is. Something called melanoma—I hope Mrs. Gamadge can spell it. I never even heard of the damn thing, but I guess it's a bitch. Well, I knew one thing: the tabloids weren't going to get ahold of this and start reporting my slow decline and taking pictures of me looking like hell. Nobody was going to stand on line in a supermarket and gloat over shots of M.L. in her last stages. So I moved fast. I called Violet La Grange—Mrs. Gamadge says you know who she was—where she lived someplace in Connecticut, and I said, "Vi, I'm going to a friend's ranch for three months to dry out and get back on my feet, and I don't want the press on my neck. Go to England till June first and be me." I sent her some cash and all my cards and identification, and I told her to be seen here and there but not too often and to keep her mouth shut. I told her where the girls would be and to send them stuff from time to time but never to write.

I stopped reading because I was remembering my feelings as I'd taken down these words. I'd been on the right track but the wrong train. There's an old expression (Sadd says one day he's going to track it to its roots), "Close, but no cigar." I read on,

I set a reasonable limit on the charge cards and told Vi that if she stuck to it, I'd give her more money when she got back and I'd tell her where to come for it. I figured

147

I'd be getting toward the end by then, and I'd add on a bonus for shutting her mouth till I was gone.

But I guess Vi suspected I was on my way out, and the greedy tramp decided to take over. She probably thought if she grabbed the kids, she'd have it made.

I looked up at Brimmer, who was nodding silently and probably thinking as I had, "I nearly got it right."

Louise said, looking into space, "But Violet hadn't figured on Celestra," the very words I'd spoken to myself. On I went.

So back she came and—hooray!—ran straight into that crazy woman's knife! You can imagine I nearly fell through the TV when I heard that! How *can* I thank the dear soul enough, Lou? I hope they aren't too hard on her. Mrs. Gamadge says they'll probably just lock her up. Will you send her a basket of fruit every Christmas from me?

I said, "Duff was in another building and didn't know of Celestra's arrival. Needless to say, I didn't tell her."

Well, to back up a bit: having fixed it up with Vi and that nice Mr. Parr, I then wrote and settled a good, hefty sum on St. Cecelia House and asked them if I could come there and die. They were wonderful. They wrote back that they'd be happy to take in kind, generous Miss Elaine Duffy. Then my dear, darling friend, I came to you with my girls, and from you, straight to St. Cecelia House.

Louise got up and went to the window. She said, "I'm not sure I can take much more."

"There isn't much more." I'd been laying the crumpled sheets on the floor beside me and now held only two. I glanced at the bottom of the last page and smiled to myself at the postscript. Of course, I wouldn't read it aloud. I said, "I was glad when she said this,

Lou, I never intended to stick you without a word. I planned to come down this week even if it meant an ambulance, and march in on you in my awful wig—we'd have had a good laugh about it—and confess all and beg you to accept the guardianship. Now Mrs. Gamadge tells me that you've accepted it anyway, which made me *die* of joy—there I go again dying all over the place. I could even say "I'll be grateful till my dying day," but that's much too soon, and I know that wherever I am, I'll be thanking you forever.

Well, Vi is probably furious that she isn't getting a bang-up funeral, all laid out in a sequined dress with an orchid pinned to her shoulder. She'd have loved that. But Elaine Duffy is happy to know that her own ashes will be spread in a birch grove in Vermont, where kids sing every morning in the summer.

I said, "She didn't sign it. Just said, 'Ask Lou to burn it.' "

Brimmer stood up. He said, "I think I'll stroll over to the pool."

He went out, and I gathered up the sheets of paper and laid them on the desk, the last one faceup.

Louise said without turning, "Will you burn it for me?"

"All right. But there's a postscript."

"What?" She looked at me, her face a blank.

"A postscript. Very personal. Read it."

She came to the desk and looked down at the letter without touching it. I said, "Read it aloud."

Louise moistened her lips and read:

> P.S.: Lou, one thing I feel bad about. Pat Brimmer. I was rotten to him. Will you be nice? Hey—I just had a knockout idea! Why the hell don't you marry him?

We began to laugh.
And she did.